# *Montana*

## LYREBIRD LAKE

## FIONA MCARTHUR

Montana

By

**Fiona McArthur**
**Lyrebird Lake Book 1**



ISBN13 9780645007602

# Montana

## CHAPTER ONE

Thank goodness Christmas was over. New Year's morning began with the faintest hint of grey shimmer on the horizon and Montana Browne gently stroked her fingers across her swollen stomach.

This would be the last New Year she would spend in the mountain hideaway before the new owners moved in. More heart-breaking than that, this would be her first New Year's morning alone, since Duncan had died.

Coffs Harbour was a long way off, holding the real world where she'd worked as a senior midwife in the busy midwifery unit. Somewhere below the white fluffy quilt thrown over the mountains, lay tucked her real house in town, shrouded like the future she couldn't see but had to have faith in.

In Coffs she had her midwifery friends, Mia and Misty and her life without Duncan.

Here at Eagle's Nest Retreat though, she was on her own. Sitting high and wild as she overlooked the distant valleys of the New England ranges and all the way to the sea. This was her farewell to the weekend retreat.

Now the sky had lightened enough to illuminate the deep drifts of mist in all the lower valleys across from the house, and she sat symbolically alone, forced to accept the empty seat beside her would always be so. Duncan was gone. Had been gone for eight months now.

The first contraction strained gently, like the tendrils of dewed spider webs that stretched the tops of the stumpy grass, and she nodded when she felt the mysterious child within herald her intentions.

She should have listened to Misty last night when her fey friend had rung to persuade her to head home early.

Montana had agreed with her two best friends that, for her child's sake, she would be safer to avoid the mountains for the last two weeks of her pregnancy, but that didn't start until a few more days.

It seemed her baby had decided to come even earlier than that, as foreseen by Misty.

Back in the tiny mountain house, Montana dialled Misty's number on the landline. Her friend might remind her of the foolishness of coming here but it would be good to share her news. And safer if things became interesting.

The phone rang three times. Then clicked. 'Hi. This is Misty. I'm out. Leave a message.'

Montana sighed. 'Misty. It's me. I'm leaving now, it's five-thirty, and I'm in early labour. Just letting you know I'm on the way in.'

She closed the house, gathered her shawl and water bottle in one hand and grasped the rail on the stairs with the other to make her way slowly down to her vehicle.

To climb into the four-wheel drive proved much more difficult than she'd expected and she chewed her lip as she started the vehicle.

The chug from the diesel engine scared a flock of lorikeets

into flight, a little like the flutter of apprehension she fought down while she waited for the engine to warm up. Two more waves of discomfort came and went in that time.

'We will be fine,' she murmured to the child within. 'Your mother is a midwife but I would prefer that you wait!' How ironic was that.

As the contractions grew closer and fiercer, a tiny frown puckered her forehead. It might not be as easy as she'd thought to drive the vehicle in early labour.

After thirty minutes of careful navigation down the misty mountain, sweat beaded her forehead, and Montana's breath fogged the windscreen with the force of the contractions. Though still able to focus on what lay around the next corner, she found it more difficult to divide her thoughts between road and birth.

The dirt track twisted and turned like the journey her baby would make within her. On an outflung clearing over-looking more mist-covered valleys she had to pull over to rest and shore up her reserves.

A pale grey wallaby and her pint-sized joey stood at the edge of the clearing. Their dark pointy faces twitched with fascination at her arrival but they didn't hop away.

Montana's labour gathered force and she glanced with despair at the distance to the valley floor. It was impossible to descend the mountain safely when she couldn't concentrate on the road.

Suddenly the tension drained from her shoulders and she slumped back. Montana let her hands fall from the wheel she'd been gripping so tightly.

So be it. She could do this. Or Misty would find her message and come.

When the vice across her belly eased she slid from the front seat and spread a rug on the damp grass. Her shawl and water beside her, she eased down to sit with her arms behind to watch the deepening of the horizon. Montana breathed out and released the tension of the drive.

Pre-dawn colours graduated from coral to pink to cerise as the sun threatened to rise through the cloud below.

When the next surge had dissolved she sighed and gazed skywards. Maybe he was looking down.

'You should be here, Duncan.' A single tear held the cold emptiness of her loss, a chill that pierced so keenly. Less than a year. A whole pregnancy since she'd seen him.

She felt the whisper of a cool breeze brush the dampness on her cheek. Gossamer soft and with a hint of warmth she didn't expect. She straightened her neck and inexplicably, she didn't feel as alone. She didn't care if she imagined him because the next pain was upon her and she needed his strength with her own to stay pliant on the waves of the contractions.

*I am here,* the wind whispered.

*You are safe.*

*I love you.*

Her shoulders eased and she gave in to the nuances of her body's prompting. In her mind it was as if she watched the descent of her baby, could squeeze her husband's hand. The waves of Mother Nature at her most powerful changed in tempo and direction and strength and suddenly the urge was upon her to ease her baby out into the world.

The sun cascaded through the clouds as the gush of water burst and flowed from within. She reached down and her baby's head glistened round and hard and hot in her hands, and then the next urge was upon her. Her baby's head rotated towards her leg, the released shoulder slid down, and then the other. Montana gasped, and breathed, and opened her mouth to moan softly as her body drove itself through the task at hand.

In long, slow seconds, her baby's body eased into the world, until, in a waterfall rush, legs and feet were followed by the tangle of cord and water. All into the fresh broken sunlight and the softly warming world.

The unmistakable sound of a newborn's first cry startled the birds as Montana reached down and gathered her daughter to her, forgetting the cord that joined them, and she laughed at the tug that reminded her that all umbilical cords were not long.

Suddenly she felt empty. Her baby was born. No longer a part of her.

A daughter. Duncan's daughter. She turned, not expecting to see him, yet so grateful she had imagined him in her time of greatest need.

The clearing was empty save for the mother wallaby and her skittish joey, and like the last of the night tendrils they too disappeared silently as the fog rolled away.

She shivered. She'd have to move. They both needed to stay warm until she could drive.

*Andy*

CHAPTER TWO

Another hairpin bend. Andy Buchanan couldn't believe he was driving his sister's vehicle on this crazy mountain road, in early morning fog, looking for Misty's widowed friend. Odd way to spend his first holiday in three years.

He'd suggested an ambulance on the phone, but his sister had vetoed that idea. 'Montana said she's in early labour. And you're a doctor. And you work in rescue in Lyrebird Lake. It's right up your alley.'

'I'm a GP, not an obstetrician,' he'd said, but refusing to help was never an option. Someone had to find the labouring woman on the mountainside and his sister had been called in to work.

'You have your diploma. A GP/OB. I feel she's fine but she needs support. Take my emergency birth pack. It even has baby wraps. I don't finish until seven and I'm stuck in labour ward or I'd go.'

Misty had 'feelings'.

Premonitions that always came true.

Like the one that had told her to check her message bank even though she was on night shift at work. His sister's friend sounded as otherworldly as his sister. Who thought driving down a mountain road this late in a first pregnancy was a good idea?

He peered through the fog as he crawled around a bend and hoped not to meet any other vehicles barring the one driven by this Montana he'd heard about for so long.

Every now and then a break in the fog showed a vista stretching all the way down to the ocean. Rolling valleys with pockets of mist, the rising sun dusting it all with gold brilliance as the fog began to break up. Incredible. He had no idea the views would be accessible from the road. Which meant, of course, cliffs where a car could drop off the edge and never be found.

Would a woman in the throes of labour veer off the road?

He never used to be a cynic but losing his darling Jess to cancer three years ago had devastated his world and left him with less optimism. He especially didn't want to deal with an obstetric emergency on a deserted mountain road.

He needed to stop thinking like that.

Montana would be fine.

If only he could find her.

Another bend and another outflung clearing. His breath hissed out. A Landcruiser, blue, parked at an angle, matching the description his sister had given him. He pulled over next to it and straightened his shoulders. Dread pooled in his stomach.

*And she'd stopped because...?*

Shaking off the dread, he opened his door and walked toward the vehicle picking up speed as he noticed a pale, dark-haired woman in the passenger side. If he wasn't mistaken she hugged a small wrapped bundle in her arms.

Good grief.

She wound down the window and he saw her shiver as if the last of the warmth in the cabin had escaped.

'You must be Montana?' He peered in and she smiled a little tiredly at him. Soft, rain-cloud grey eyes like velvet. Dark hair tied back. Tiredness under her eyes in a grey smudge. She had a right to be tired. He couldn't believe she'd birthed here.

Alone.

On a freakin' mountain.

'Yes, I'm Montana. I gather Misty sent you?'

He nodded. 'I'm Andy, her brother. She's on duty, in the labour ward. Couldn't get away.' He looked across at the top of her baby's head snuggled into her chest. With blankets over both it made a fair mountain of cloth, yet he still felt the need to ask. 'Are you warm enough?'

'Yes. Except for my feet.'

He couldn't believe her absolute tranquillity. Not all he could expect from a woman who had just given birth. Without support. He tried to see the baby's face. 'And who is this?'

She shifted a fold of blanket so he could see a tiny wrinkled face and then Montana smiled. He felt the impact of that smile, that curve of her lips and the adoration of her baby in her grey eyes, sending unexpected warmth right down to his hiking boots. Somewhere inside him a cold clump of ice shifted in his chest like a kicked coal from an outback campfire. A fire someone had thought dead.

'This is my daughter, Dawn.'

The serenity in her voice wrapped around him like the fog he'd just driven through to get here. Except not cool, not cool at all. She'd come to terms with the unexpected events, he thought with a flash of insight, and so must he. She was alive and the baby had mewled. He leaned forward to see more.

'Hello, Dawn.' He noted the thatch of dark hair against Montana, the healthy pink baby cheeks, and the baby snuffled as if in answer. Dawn? 'I think I can guess what time she arrived.'

His smile faded and his training reminded him this woman had been without assistance at a critical time. He framed the question as delicately as he could. 'Any problems you need help with?'

'No, thank you.' She glanced at him and he heard the humour behind her voice when she spoke. 'Third stage complete and I'm not bleeding or seem to be damaged. My baby has fed.'

How could she be amused? She should be hysterical. He didn't like the way he was so conscious of his sister's friend. He didn't look at other women; he'd loved his wife. Andy corrected himself. He *still* loved his wife. Maybe it was empathy. *Of course.* He remembered now she was a widow. He understood and felt for her recent loss.

They were on the side of a mountain, for heaven's sake, and she'd just had a baby. Alone. He felt sorry for her. That was it.

He concentrated on the things he was good at. Practical things. Things that didn't include analysing his emotions. 'Right, then. Let's get you out of here.' He glanced around to decide where to reverse the vehicle.

Montana's voice floated across the distance between them, gentle, as if explaining to a child. 'We have to wait for the fog on the road to clear further down before we go.'

He hadn't reckoned on resistance to rescue. 'I managed to get here.'

'That's lovely.' And she smiled that indulgent smile that made his neck prickle under his collar. 'I'm not risking my daughter in a drive down the mountain with a man I don't know. Or, not until the mist is gone completely.' She added, 'Even if the man driving is a doctor and does rescue for a living.'

So Misty had told her about him. What else had she shared with this woman?

The inflexible set of her chin and the tilt of her fine-boned face should have exasperated him, but inexplicably he could feel himself bend to her wishes, like the tree above him was bent by time spent in the buffeting climate.

*Now* she wanted to be sensible? Andy shrugged, in the big picture, both were well, the birth was done, if it was important to her. So be it. 'Fine. We'll wait.' He paused while they both pondered how long that would be. 'Would you like a cup of tea?'

He saw her eyes widen and his mouth twitched as he tried to contain his amusement. Ha!

Deadpan, he gave the choices as he watched her face. 'Earl Grey, breakfast, peppermint or jasmine tea?' He did rescue. He'd packed a thermos. Two hot water bottles. And tea bags lived in his glove box. Countless people had blessed him for such items.

'You have choices in tea?' A tiny frown marred her forehead as if she wasn't sure if he was joking. A look of hope. 'Jasmine?'

'Fine. I'll rustle that up shortly.' He pulled one of the hot water bottles he'd borrowed from his sister's house from his coat pocket and showed it to her.

'Perhaps you'd like this. For those cold feet.' He touched the handle of her car door and raised his brows. 'May I?'

When she nodded he opened the door and tucked the warm rubber bottle under the blanket against her feet. Such little feet. Perfect and elegant.

Slim, shapely ankles, too, but he liked her feet. He heard

her sigh with pleasure as he stepped back, and that dragged his mind away from her toes. He had a foot fetish? What was wrong with him this morning?

The air seemed colder now that he'd moved back away from her. 'Sure you're warm enough? I have a great heater in my car.'

She tugged the blanket closer around her neck. 'That seems sensible. Perhaps you could heat your car first? I could hand you Dawn to keep snug while I do a bit of a tidy with myself?'

A good plan, he thought. As long as she didn't faint when she stood. He'd make sure she was steady as soon as he had the car warm. 'Don't go anywhere,' he deadpanned. 'I'll be right back.'

## CHAPTER THREE

So this was Misty's big brother from Queensland.

Montana watched him walk away. A tall, lean man even taller than Duncan, he'd towered over her door and now moved away with unusual grace for such a big man. Andy resembled his sister with his dark auburn hair and green eyes, but there was no doubt he held the Y chromosome. Nothing feminine there. Even to the stubble of red that said he'd had no time to shave before he'd come to rescue her.

His voice was different from Duncan's not as deep or careful with enunciation but it held the same timbre of quiet authority underscored with warmth and caring. That must be why she felt so safe.

Somehow it seemed appropriate that Misty's four-wheel drive had pulled up next to hers in the early morning light and, strangely, it even seemed right to have her brother come to rescue her. Although they'd never met, he did not feel like a stranger.

Minutes drifted peacefully and then he was back. 'The car is heating up nicely. Shall I take Dawn?'

He held out his arms and she saw he'd unwrapped a small

blanket and a tiny warm beanie from another hot-water bottle.

It didn't surprise her. Misty being known for her uncannily accurate premonitions. 'Misty must have suspected Dawn would arrive.'

Andy nodded. 'Although when she told me "early labour", she then said, "take the baby wraps".' He smiled. A nice smile. As warm and open as his sisters but definitely male. 'I've learnt to believe her when she "feels" something.'

'Is it a family trait?' Montana could see he was proud of his fey sister. She liked that pride. Another thing she liked about him.

He smiled crookedly and the way he curved his firm mouth made him more a person in his own right and less Misty's brother. 'Sometimes I'm accused of uncanny "luck" if we're searching for someone, but not with the precision and clarity of Misty.'

He pulled the soft bonnet over Dawn's hair as if he'd beanied a baby many times. He rolled her little body in the blanket as he peeled her away from Montana's skin so that the cold air wouldn't distress her. Dawn didn't whimper.

Even Duncan, an obstetrician, hadn't been that adept at handling babies. Montana stopped that thought in its tracks with a stern shake of her head. She really had to stop comparing people to her darling Duncan. It was neither fair nor constructive.

Cold air whispered against her skin and she hugged the blanket tight as she watched him wrap Dawn in another warm shawl. Then he tucked the baby against his chest, and flattened the blanket back firmly around Montana with his other hand. He must have seen her shiver.

Dawn grizzled and he whispered something she couldn't

catch. His cheek rested against the tiny head while he carried her to the warmth of the car.

Montana frowned at how easy they looked together and decided she'd had enough huddling to keep warm.

Her warm feet felt good and she slipped the bottle up to tuck into her now loose trousers, hot water on tap when she was ready, and it would keep her stomach warm until then. She pulled her shirt together where she'd opened it to keep her daughter snug against her skin.

Andy returned without Dawn before Montana could climb out of the car. 'She's tucked safe on the seat. Can't fall. I just want to make sure you're fine.' He gestured with his hand. 'When you stand.'

'Thank you.' She slid gingerly out and his hand was close but not touching. She drew in a deep breath and her head stayed clear. 'Yes. I'm fine.'

He moved back. 'If you're sure. I'll turn my back.'

She laughed softly. 'You watch Dawn. I'll go around the other side of the car by myself, thank you.'

Two minutes later, after she'd communed with nature, and had almost groaned with the sheer bliss of hot water from the rubber bottle to wash her face and hands, she'd refastened her clothes and tidied as best she could. She crossed to Misty's car and her daughter.

Dawn dozed happily tucked into Andy's arm and Montana stilled him with a raised hand as he went to lean across to open the passenger door. She slid in. 'Don't move. She's settled.'

He had the cup holders out on the dashboard and each held a steaming cup of tea that caused twin puffs of condensation on the windshield.

'The tea smells wonderful.' Inhaling the aroma, she gathered the cup in her fingers to divert her silly mind away from the man in the driver's seat. A man thoughtful and practical enough to bring tea-making supplies. A man who looked totally at ease with a newborn in his arms.

How brilliant that Andy had known instinctively not to fuss about her or about Dawn's sudden arrival. Even Duncan would have panicked at the thought of birthing here on the mountain.

Montana sipped her tea slowly and let the past hour fall from her shoulders.

They sat silently for some time, quietness easy between them, and Montana may even have dozed.

When she opened her eyes he was looking at her. Not staring, just an appraisal to see if she was fine. She couldn't remember when she'd felt so comfortable in a stranger's company.

'Were you frightened?' His words were soft and acknowledged something powerful and amazing had happened that morning. And again, for her, there was that pleasure in his lack of censure.

She smiled at the bundle that was her daughter and shook her head. Suddenly it was important he understand that she wasn't reckless with her daughter's life. 'I wasn't expecting it to happen so quickly. I thought I could get to the hospital, but I couldn't drive any more, not safely anyway, and when I stopped it all happened as it should.'

'So I see. Fortunate.' he said quietly.

She met his eyes thoughtfully. 'I won't say I was lucky it all went well, because I have always believed a woman is designed to give birth without complications. I was just not unlucky, as some women are.'

He seemed to be pondering her statement; not quite a disagreement but not sure he agreed, perhaps? He didn't say anything. Instead he flattened his chin against his chest and squinted at the baby snuggled like a possum into him. 'What do you think Dawn weighs?'

Montana looked proudly across at her daughter and smiled again. 'Maybe six pounds. Say two and a half thousand grams. She's almost three weeks early but she's vigorous.'

'She's perfect.'

'I know,' she said. They smiled at each other in mutual admiration for Montana's baby. This time Montana was the first to look away, aware of that ease between them, which was unexpected. That was okay. The occasion was special enough for odd feelings.

He reached over to the back of the seat and lifted a small lunch holder. 'Would you like some sandwiches?'

'Actually, I'm starving.' The man was so practical. 'You've prepared well.'

'Least I can do. I'd rather have been here half an hour earlier.'

She unwrapped the sandwich and bit into it with relish. 'My favourite,' she said around a mouthful of bread and ham and pickles. 'Labour is hungry work.'

He smiled at her. A lovely smile and she smiled back.

'Is there anything you don't have?' she said just before the next bite, and the words hung in the air between them.

He looked out at the mist below them in the valley and she felt his sudden pain. Heck. He'd lost his wife. She knew now what that felt like. His voice came out a little more brusquely than she expected. 'I don't have a trailer to bring your truck down with us, but I'll come back and get it later.'

Despite that good comeback, an awkward silence hung between them now where before it had been peaceful. The mist had begun to dissipate lower down the mountain. Time to go.

This interlude from the world would be over, and she'd be

tucked up in a ward bed with Misty and her other friend, Mia, fussing over her in the maternity section of their hospital. All the staff would pass by and look in, and everything would be as it should be.

Except Duncan wouldn't be there.

All the things she hadn't said and couldn't share with Duncan would never be spoken and she needed to accept that. But she dreaded each day in her home environment, which had become so entrenched in loss and memories.

Her husband wouldn't be in the ward where she'd first seen him. Wouldn't be in any of the familiar places where they'd spent the last years of his life together.

How did one cope with this feeling of desolation?

Or of the guilt-ridden feeling that Duncan had let her down somehow by dying? Left her to mother their child and manage everything that comes with.

What of the fact that a stranger had been the first man to see Dawn and not Duncan?

Her eyes stung and a tear rolled down her cheek. 'I don't want to go to the hospital.' The dam she'd been holding back for months burst. 'Actually, I don't ever want to go back to that hospital. I don't even want to go back to my house in town, which is ridiculous as I don't have the energy to organise a clean break.'

The understanding in his green eyes nearly triggered the tears again.

She bit her lip, swiped at her eyes, and shook her head. 'This is not like me. I'm sorry. I have no option. Ignore what I just said.'

'Anyone would think you'd had a big morning,' he quipped gently, and the compassion in his voice told her he understood. He really did understand.

Andy slid his arm across the seat and around her shoulder

and squeezed. Despite the fact that she didn't know him it felt good to be hugged. Comforting.

'It must be hard without your husband,' he said. 'I felt the same when my wife died.'

'Misty told me.'

'Did she say how I'd almost gone off the rails? Left everything to get away? Had to escape.'

No, she hadn't mentioned that. 'It's harder than anything in the world,' she said, 'and sometimes I'm almost angry with him for leaving.' Montana lifted her face to his. Her eyes shimmered with loss and she saw the acknowledgment.

'I remember that feeling,' he said. He squeezed her shoulder. 'What happened to Duncan?'

She shook her head. Still barely believing it had happened so fast. 'The tenth of April. It was an aneurysm. There was no warning. Duncan went to bed smiling and never woke up. He was thirty-five and didn't even know he would be a father.'

The silence lengthened as they both reflected on their losses. Thank goodness he didn't rush in with condolences because she hated that. Hated the words and having to respond and each regret underlined her loss with another stab of pain.

Finally, he said, 'It was a tragedy. Though he has given you a beautiful daughter and he will live on through her.'

She nodded. 'I know. But I don't ever want to hurt like that again.'

'Amen to that.' Andy sighed, a soft exhalation filled with understanding. 'People kept telling me that time is a great healer, but the early years are painful and something I never want to do again.'

Months had been bad. Years sounded terrible. She had to do it with a daily reminder in Dawn, but she would survive.

'I have a direction in my life now with the hospital at Lyrebird Lake. Time has given me that consolation.'

'And I have Dawn.' Yes. She had Dawn.

Andy squeezed Montana's shoulders once more and then let his arm drop. 'I'll get your things and put them in my car.'

'I want to go home.' Her voice firmed. 'Not to the hospital.'

He looked at her. Didn't seem surprised. 'Fine. I'm sure your own personal midwives will arrive as soon as they hear you are home.'

He smiled and Montana found she could smile, if a little tremulously, back. He was right.

Of course she didn't have to go to the hospital.

Mia and Misty would make sure she was well looked after.

*Andy*

CHAPTER FOUR

Andy spent the week of his working holiday completing the tasks he'd set himself.

First, he'd driven the four hours east to Brisbane, for some business meetings, then five hours south to Coffs. The hospital had offered extra operating hours as a locum surgeon to refresh his skillset. This was his first time down here and he'd been kindly received.

Great to know because the occasional disaster did crop up at Lyrebird Lake, and they lacked back-up. The tiny hospital he'd run to after his wife died had captured his loyalty and championship. Ensuring his skills remained current, when he didn't get a lot of practice until said emergencies arrived, was part of the bargain he made to himself.

Second, he lost no opportunity to promote the idea of transfer to Lyrebird Lake for any health professional at the hospital in Coffs Harbour, anyone who would listen and might be remotely interested in relocating to a smaller hospital for work just over the Queensland border, though out west a bit.

The Lake needed staff if it was to move into the bright future the new mine would bring, and this was a great opportunity to scout for potential colleagues. Andy had sworn he would do his best to help find staff. If he didn't, the hospital would be downgraded even further and the funding on offer would be diverted to the base hospital, one hundred and eighty kilometres away.

That would happen over his dead body.

And the third thing he did was try not to think too much about Montana Browne.

His holiday was over, though it hadn't been intended for relaxation or dalliance, it had allowed him to catch up with his only sister, refresh skills and scout for other staff. He hadn't relaxed but his mind had dallied. On Montana.

Since Montana's baby had arrived early, he'd spent a lot of time in and out of the new mother's house after work, because Misty had taken on the cooking and shopping role for Montana in some pre-arranged, pre-birth deal the girls had going.

The other friend, Mia, had been assigned washing and housework, so Andy had offered to mow the lawns and trim the hedges before he left.

He didn't mind. It gave him a chance to watch Montana, a pastime he suspected he could become addicted to. The play of emotions across her face. The lift of her lips when he said something that amused her.

He liked to watch her quiet, calm competence but today she seemed edgy. Her easy smile had turned to tense and serious. He'd only seen her like this one other time. On the mountain, when she'd said she didn't want to go home. Funny how that had stuck in his mind ever since.

Something wasn't right with Montana today.

It was a typical three-women-and-extra-brother afternoon

at Montana's house and he found it all strangely poignant that it was the last he would be present at.

His sister crooned and stroked Dawn's downy cheek as she whispered to the tiny baby in her arms. 'You are beautiful,' she said. 'Yes, you are.'

Andy heard the words, but his attention was on Montana as she rested back in the lounge with the cup of jasmine tea he'd made while she fielded the barrage of questions Mia seemed obsessed with.

'You sure you didn't have a premonition? You didn't suspect you'd go into labour?'

'No premonition. I leave that to Misty.'

Montana's quiet voice drifted across the room to him and he saw her glance at him but she didn't smile.Why did he need her to smile?

'And to Andy,' she finished, and he savoured the way she said his name.

He should go. Get out of this hens' party and think about packing to head home. He still had a heap of shopping to do before he flew back tomorrow morning and if he went back to the Lake without the special ingredients Louisa, his housekeeper, had requested, he was a dead man.

He just couldn't seem to tear his eyes away from Montana today. The day he'd met her replayed like a favourite movie in his mind. He could still see her alone in an isolated clearing on the side of a mountain surrounded by mist — a woman as Zen as a monk after giving birth alone.

She'd avoided the hospital as she'd wanted, though he admitted she had two willing experts in his sister and Mia.

Here in her own home, even with her new baby, he'd never seen her succumb to any sort of anxiety, until now.

He kept remembering how serene she'd been when he'd first arrived to bring her back. That serenity was missing, and he didn't think it was just the fact that Mia was hounding her again, but maybe it was.

'Mia, leave her alone.' Although he said it quietly, his voice cut across the room and the three women turned towards him.

Dawn began to cry and Misty carried her across to her mother as she glared at her brother.

He was in trouble now. Andy smiled what he hoped was a conciliatory smile. Misty glared right back.

All three women could indicate displeasure with their eyes but his sister won hands down. Their mother had been the same, but Misty would have been too young to remember that.

'Sorry. I didn't mean to startle everyone. Forget it.' His sister would flay him for upsetting the baby but he was more worried about upsetting Montana.

Maybe his sister could help. 'Can I see you for a minute, Misty, please?'

Misty shrugged and Montana raised one eyebrow mockingly as if to say he'd picked the wrong household to assert his authority, but he could see she was fine with him at least.

Misty waved him to the kitchen where they could see the others but not hear the conversation.

'Sorry.' Useful deflection. 'Just wanted to ask you if you think it's a good thing Montana stays here when it obviously makes her so sad.'

As a spur-of-the-moment diversion, it had come with a lot of thought.

Misty frowned and tilted her head as if to peer inside his mind. He hated when she did that because a lot of the time she could guess what he was thinking, even when he didn't know what he was thinking himself.

'What choice does she have?' She spoke slowly, watching

him intently, as if trying to work out his angle. She probably thought he was interested in Montana. Well, he was — but not like that!

He'd been there when Montana said she didn't want to come back to this house, this town, anywhere near the hospital.

'Montana could come back to Lyrebird Lake with me.'

He waited. ' Tomorrow. As a change of scenery. She said she didn't want to go back to the hospital here at Coffs Harbour to work. The Lake will need to replace a midwife and an evening supervisor in a couple of months. She could just rest and settle into the place until then. Maybe she could fill those positions later until she decides what she wants to do.'

Misty's eyes narrowed. 'You'd have to talk to her about that yourself. It's too soon to drive all that way with a new baby, and she hates small planes. How would you get her there?'

'I haven't thought the details through yet. I wanted to get your thoughts before talking to Montana.'

She shook her head slowly, thoughtfully. She didn't seem as negative as he'd thought she would be. It wasn't that dumb. And it was away from the memories. He knew how much that had helped him.

'I can't imagine Montana wanting to head to the back of beyond with a new baby,' Misty said finally.

'It's the country, not remote desert. There's no strangeness in that,' he said.

'There is the problem of leaving everyone you know at a time you need them most.' Misty screwed her face up that he could be so dense. He wondered who was going to miss who?

'But she said she wanted to get away. Now.' He'd be there for her and so would Louisa and Ned, the older couple who had been his salvation when he'd come to the lake, broken, after Jess's death. Sometimes strangers helped. 'She'd know me. There's a town full of people who would help.'

'Strangers!' As if she'd heard his thought. Misty's disbelief came out a little forced? Did she too, see some advantage for Montana in his suggestion?

He lowered his voice. 'Maybe that's what she needs right now.'

Montana drifted across the room towards them and he watched her approach. Misty looked pointedly at her brother. 'Ask her.'

He grimaced. It wasn't how he would have chosen to broach the subject, but something told him Montana had got the gist of their discussion anyway and maybe postponing this wasn't helping. Even from the beginning he'd never doubted her powers of observation.

At least her expression could be construed as interested, not wary.

Here goes, he thought. 'I wondered if you might like to come home with me tomorrow. For a change, away from everything for the first few weeks of Dawn's life. A change of scene, Montana. Not a commitment.'

'With what aim?' she asked mildly.

'Maybe a job if you like the place, but later. When and if you're ready, to stay up my way. We have vacancies we can't fill at the cottage hospital.'

'Go on?' Montana said.

She watched his face as he spoke and he hoped he made sense. 'I think I've mentioned I live in a rambling old house with tons of room and a housekeeper who spoils us. There's another semi-retired doctor plus any locums that can come for a week or two to give us relief. It's quiet but not isolated.'

'Quiet sounds good.' Inclined her head a fraction as if to say keep going.

He glanced briefly at the bassinet by the window, where Dawn now slept. 'You and Dawn could share with us for as long as you like, or even have your own cottage, as there are a few on the hospital grounds if that would suit you better.'

She looked more receptive than he'd hoped. 'We'll be looking for another midwife and an evening supervisor when the current one retires in a few months. Misty told me you have a management degree and I thought you might be interested in a fresh start.'

Misty watched, but both ignored her, as Montana considered the idea.

Misty might have expected Montana to turn him down but he'd say Montana actually looked relieved he'd asked her.

She fixed her calm eyes on him. 'I've heard you say you don't deliver babies at the Lake,' she said quietly, and raised her finely arched brows. 'Is that hospital policy or just because of the lack of midwives?'

'Occasionally we have babies. There's myself and Ned, the semi-retired GP I live with, but we only have one midwife on staff with any obstetric experience. We catch unexpected babies when we have to but send the rest to the regional hospital because that's where the skill base is.'

Her brows went up.

Of course. that's where her interest would lie, he thought, and wondered how he could turn that to his advantage.

'That is something we expect might have to change as the town grows.' He shrugged and grinned. 'If you can convince a few of your friends to migrate north, that would be good, too. I'm happy to listen to ideas.'

'Good to know,' she said.

He tried not to project the exhilaration he usually only felt when he'd accomplished a difficult surgery or diagnosed an elusive condition. Or landed a beautiful fish.

'A midwifery-led clinic and caseload, you mean?' Her chin was up and he could feel her intensity.

'Perhaps, though you'd have to explain caseload midwifery more fully to me.' A new service for the lake would be well received by the town. He just might have the carrot she needed. 'I know you've been involved with the stand-alone centre at Coffs.'

'Women-centred care is more common now since women consumers have documented what they want. I'd be happy to clarify the concepts for you.' She chewed her bottom lip. 'How long would I have to stay if I came up and just had a look?'

'No ties.' He didn't want to scare her off, for a variety of reasons. Once she'd seen the place and the potential he'd seen, she'd be interested. He hoped. She had a lot to offer and he pressed his advantage, unable to believe his luck that she was considering the idea.

'The current Manager would be delighted to answer any questions you had. We could say you're visiting, if you like, then if you decided to go home no one would be any wiser.'

'A freeloader?' She wasn't happy with that and he wondered if she'd ever taken anything for nothing.

'With a view to helping us out in the future. Or a consultant on ideas for the hospital. That's not freeloading. Rest for as long as you need. A few months at least. Lots of things run on a barter system at the Lake. We'll sort something out. It's not easy to get staff, so if you stayed to work short or long term, we'd be fine with that.'

'Babysitting?' She'd changed. He couldn't pick when it had happened, but she'd lost the anxious look she'd had all morning. Now she looked engaged. He could see the shift and he liked the new light in her grey eyes. It was beginning to feel as if they were the only two in the room and he liked that as well...Perhaps too much.

'You have my attention,' she said quietly.

He thought of Louisa, his housekeeper, and how much she'd adore Dawn. 'Our housekeeper is a grandmother whose grandkids live away. She'd be in seventh heaven with Dawn and might just want to adopt you both. I suspect she would happily look after Dawn if you needed her to.'

Why did it matter so much that this woman would come? Plenty of others had declined and he'd been philosophical about them.

'Thank you for asking me,' was all she said. 'I'd like to think about it.'

He watched her exchange a look with Misty and his sister frowned. Was that a good look or a bad look? He'd done all he could. He nodded and moved across to apologise to Mia for barking.

# Montana

## CHAPTER FIVE

Montana watched his progress across the room before she turned to Misty.

She needed this. The memories everywhere she looked were crushing her. 'I'd like to go with your brother to Lyrebird Lake.'

Misty frowned. 'You made that decision fast.' But the lack of surprise in her friend's voice made Montana smile.

'I've been a mess, trying to decide whether to ask him all morning. I knew they had staffing problems but it will be weeks before I'll want to think about work. With somewhere to stay, it's the perfect answer.'

'Perfect answer to what?' Misty asked ruefully. 'You have everything here.' She included Mia in an encompassing gesture that took in her home, her neighbourhood, perhaps the whole town. 'You have us. All of us.'

'That's true,' Montana agreed, 'and that part will be hard. I love you guys, and I will miss you, but there's too much pain here.'

Very softly her friend said, 'I know.'

She met Misty's eyes. 'I need to get away and start life

afresh with Dawn. I'm not looking to replace Duncan, just looking for somewhere everyone doesn't panic about what to say to me in case they upset me. I'll never forget Duncan, can't imagine being with another man, but I need to be a whole person for my daughter, and I can't do that here.'

'Fair enough, but don't decide now. Wait a few hours.' Misty leaned in and hugged her. Spoke quietly, earnestly. 'He leaves tomorrow. It's going to happen fast and you might wake up and wonder what you've done.'

'I know. But that's a risk I have to take. I would be in safe hands.' Montana looked across at Andy, where he sat laughing with Mia. He made her laugh too, and that wasn't an easy thing to do, but she needed that as much as a change of environment. The past year had been so devoid of laughter. 'Will you help me?'

'Of course.' Misty peered at her watch as she tried to calculate how much time they had. 'You never know. I might turn up for a visit there one day myself.'

'That would be the best. You'd have to bring Mia. We'd have fun, though her boyfriend wouldn't like that.' The two women smiled and they both knew Mia's relationship had its rocky moments. They both considered Mia had jumped into that relationship way too fast and it wasn't an easy one.

It took Montana a while to come to grips with the fact that not only did Andy own a small aircraft, but he would be the pilot if she wanted to avoid a two-day car trip with a newborn.

She'd always had a reluctance to fly and the idea of a tiny two-seater plane with her daughter was right up there in nightmare territory. If she hadn't had such unexpected confidence in Andy a confidence grounded in how he'd handled their unusual first meeting on the mountainside she would have pulled out.

She eased herself stiffly into the cramped seat, quickly breathed in and out a couple of times. She could do this. Or so she thought until she tried to secure her seat belt.

It wouldn't latch into place.

Her fingers fumbled.

Her breathing grew shallow.

She tried again one-handed with Dawn against her chest and then again with slightly more desperation until the door beside her opened and the woodsy aftershave she'd begun to associate with Andy drifted past her nose.

'May I?' He looked down at her with a reassuring smile and she remembered why she'd decided to go with this man. Along with that enticing scent, he brought calm and competence.

She sighed and relaxed, and at her nod Andy clicked her belt into place and then secured the tiny strap around Dawn that threaded between mother and daughter like a leather umbilical cord for emergencies.

It meant she was joined again to her daughter and she liked the idea. She wondered who would be drawing reassurance from whom in the coming flight. Thank God Andy was there to look after both of them.

Then Andy climbed into the other side of the plane and squeezed his big frame down next to her. She could feel the warmth from his body like a soothing shield and she enjoyed feeling slightly safer until she remembered his presence meant they were close to take-off.

Oh, boy, she thought grimly, and concentrated on his strong hands as they caressed the controls. An unexpected wish to feel those fingers squeeze her hand in comfort made her twist to stare out the window.

'You okay?'

She heard his voice and schooled her features into a semblance of calm control before she turned back. 'Fine,' she lied, apparently convincingly because he looked across at her and grinned.

He nodded and resumed his flight preparations. She chewed her lip while he talked to the flight control tower and then it was too late to change her mind because the little Cessna had begun to taxi in an ungainly rattle down the Coffs Harbour runway.

Another small plane in front of them waited for take-off and she watched in sick fascination as it lined up and then hurtled away from them before it climbed precariously high into the sky.

Their plane would have to do that. She swallowed the fear in her throat. She wished irrationally that Dawn would be less settled and whimper or do something to distract her, but her daughter snoozed on regardless.

Andy positioned the plane on the white line of the runway and the engine built in noise until it seemed to scream — a little like the noise Montana wanted to make but couldn't — and her nerves stretched.

He looked across at her and flashed his white teeth and she realised, belatedly, the kick he got from this. Huh. Who knew? She acknowledged him with an attempted smile that felt more like a grimace, then returned to the only thing she could do as she breathed in and out. She prayed.

Breathing was a good thing and improved the lightness in her head, at least. Of course, praying could be helpful if divine intervention was required.

He released the brakes and the plane began its thunder

down the runway. When she risked a look the tarmac beside her blurred. Suddenly the noise changed and her stomach plummeted and she realised they were in the air as the ground dropped woozily below her window.

*OhmyGod.* She turned her head away and closed her eyes.

Obviously Dawn travelled better than her mother. She remained sound asleep. Montana tried to think of something different that rhymed with doom and gloom and boom.

She moistened her lips and risked opening one eye.

They'd levelled out and Andy looked so disgustedly relaxed. And happy. Disgustingly happy. She opened her other eye.

She'd talk about the weather. Pilots were on top of the weather thing she reckoned. 'So, do you have emergency supplies in this thing and a homing beacon?' That wasn't what she'd meant to say.

Andy smiled. 'GPS tracker and, yes, we have basic emergency supplies. Today we even have English muffins, ginger marmalade and Norfolk punch as extras for my housekeeper and jasmine tea for you. But despite the size of the plane, we're safe.'

'Right.' Sure, she thought.

He glanced at her sleeping daughter. 'Dawn isn't worried.'

Montana looked down at her. 'Hmm. She has less imagination than I have.'

'Wimp.'

His eyes danced and she noticed the little brown flecks through the green of his irises, before frowning at the unfairness of the comment. 'Hey, if I was a wimp, I wouldn't be here.'

The hundred-watt smile he sent her way warmed the ice around her heart and made her forget she and Dawn were in a fragile capsule a mile above the earth. Now it felt more like she floated in the air without support amongst the clouds outside her window. Heady stuff. Probably oxygen deprivation.

'That's true. You are not a wimp. Well done.' His words continued to warm that cold spot she'd had in her chest for far too long, though it was probably just reactionary euphoria that they hadn't died on take-off.

He changed the subject and began to recite anecdotes about the older doctor he lived with, and by the time they were nearly there she had acclimatised to the concept of flight, with Andy at least.

Montana's first sight of Lyrebird Lake as they broke through the low cloud surprised and delighted her. It even looked like a lyrebird. Then the engine changed pitch and they were coming in to land. No more just the three of them. Destination time. She gulped.

She didn't know anyone in this town except Andy. What had she been thinking to leave everything she knew behind and literally take off with her week-old baby and a man she barely knew? Even if he was the most reassuring man she'd ever known.

The grey of the water on the lake reflected the grey of the clouds that had dogged most of their journey and nerves hit. Her spirits plummeted.

What if it didn't work out?

What if Dawn cried every night and kept the whole household awake?

What if she lost this rapport with Andy that she relied on so much?

What on earth was she doing?

# Andy

## CHAPTER SIX

'You still with me?'

Andy felt the change in Montana's mood as soon as Lyrebird Lake came into view, even though she tried to hide it. He wanted to reach over and squeeze her hand and reassure her that everything would work out, but despite the way his sister and her friends hugged each other so openly and regularly, he was wary of encroaching on Montana.

He knew why. Andy struggled with the idea he was thinking of touching another woman after Jess.

He was way too aware of this woman, but everything he'd done to try and change that awareness hadn't worked. And now they'd be living in the same house. He needed to draw a line that he wouldn't cross. Unnecessary touching was the core of it.

He was more than happy to help when he could, but it didn't mean he had to try and fix all her problems.

It could be just her distrust of flying — lots of people weren't comfortable in small planes — and he admired the way she'd overcome that fear without fuss or demands. But he had an idea it was more than that.

She was independent. He was that way himself so that shouldn't bother him, but he wanted her to know he was available as a shoulder to lean on. As a brother, of course.

He'd brought Montana here for a job. He was ecstatic with her extensive resume of midwifery credentials and the administrative degree he needed.

Bringing her with him was all business.

Not personal.

He could handle it. Could keep it in the friends-zone. Keep it professional. He'd drawn the line and he was okay with that.

He watched her slender fingers slide gently over Dawn's hair and wondered who drew comfort from whom as she cuddled her baby close.

'I'm okay,' she said. 'I just had a minute of panic.'

Only a minute was amazing.

She stared out the window at the expanse of water below and he leant across to point things out because it directed his thoughts away from the personal. He was keeping that line firmly in place.

Besides, he'd always loved this view and he hoped she could see the beauty below despite the scar of new development near the lake.

A scattering of established houses along the shore added to the town which sat nestled under a set of hills. 'See the hills and the lookout? We have great bushwalks and even a small waterfall up there.'

She looked. 'I love waterfalls.'

There it was. 'There's the hospital,' he said. 'That's all in the hospital grounds.' He pointed out the largest tin-roofed building and a scattering of smaller buildings spreading out from it. 'The building across the park is our house.'

Montana inclined her head towards the town below. 'The

town is smaller than I anticipated.' Her voice seemed smaller than before and a moment's panic had him hoping she didn't want to turn around and go home.

'It's tiny compared to Coffs Harbour, that's true, but it's full of good people.' He wanted her to feel comfortable and feel the potential he saw in the area himself.

The hospital needed her.

He needed her...in a professional capacity.

'We have a large feeder district but anyone with a complicated medical condition would still be shipped out. Admissions to the hospital are fairly simple and mostly brief. If it's not simple, it's gone. But if we expand our services, that would change with the needs of the mine population.'

She nodded. 'Lyrebird Lake is an unusual name. Is it because of the shape of the lake or because you have lyrebirds?'

He'd heard different versions. 'Depends who you ask. I guess it's the shape of the lake. We're pretty far north as a habitat. There's not much rainforest around here, though we do have some patches of wet forest which would make it possible.'

She nodded. 'They are supposed to look like a small turkey with a tail. Has anyone ever seen one here?'

'Not that I know of. I've never seen one although I've heard some pretty strange noises in the bush so I guess I could have heard one. Apparently the lyrebird can copy another bird's song, or an animal, or even man-made noises like chainsaws and crying babies.'

She smiled. 'That would be a mother's nightmare. One crying baby is enough.'

'Ned says there's a local myth that those who have suffered will be rewarded when the lyrebird visits. No visitations for me in the three years I've been here, and I think he's pulling my leg.'

She smiled at his sceptical amusement. 'So why are you here?'

He shrugged. 'Lyrebird or not, the lake healed me, and I think it could help you too.' He looked across at her and hoped she realised he genuinely believed that.

'And?' She wanted to know more about him.

'The people are legitimate, as is their need, and you can't stay immune to their warmth,' he said. 'I appreciate that after living in the city.'

She inclined her head so maybe she did understand. 'Which hospital did you work in?' she asked, and for the first time in a long time he didn't mind answering.

'The year after my wife died I spent it in the emergency department at Sydney General. U and O they called it. Understaffed and overwhelmed.' His voice lowered as he remembered. 'You know what it's like. Extreme hours, no emotional involvement with patients, just save them or lose them. I was happy to do that as I built up a big wall to hide behind. I couldn't see myself becoming more clinical and distanced from humanity.'

'I don't want to do that, either,' she said softly, 'but I could see how it can happen. Sometimes I want to push people who knew Duncan and I as a couple far away. Even new, young families I've known for years, who have two parents for their baby. I push them away too.'

'Exactly that,' he said. 'Misty and the friends I started to alienate...They saw it long before I did.' He'd been horrid and taciturn after his wife died it was a wonder he had any friends left. 'My colleagues ganged up on me and suggested I resign. They told me about Ned, the Lake's semi-retired GP, and how he needed help for a few months until he found a new partner. He's has macular degeneration and I've been here ever since.'

He thought back over the last couple of years and how his mindset had altered for the better. 'I've grown to love it here and I'm committed to providing the medical needs of the community. If those needs adjust then the hospital will darned well adjust too. You can help there if it inspires you to.'

He pointed to the north. 'It made things interesting when the mine opened up twenty kilometres away, and now the farmland is selling faster than the local government can subdivide. We have our first restaurant in town.'

'A real restaurant in town? Very flash.' She smiled, probably at the pride in his voice, and he laughed.

'It is for us.' He'd take her there one day. Angelo would love Montana.

He went on. 'The hospital will get busier and the idea of a midwifery-led unit is not as far-fetched as you might imagine. There is a core of women in town who are very progressive and well-read on their rights. They'd love women-centred care.'

She tilted her head. 'And I thought you were just saying that to tempt me.'

He smiled and tried not to think about who was tempting whom, because that wasn't part of the plan. 'Now, why would I do that?'

She looked at him thoughtfully. 'I don't know. Perhaps you recognised my symptoms from your own past or maybe —' she paused and considered him '—maybe you just wanted someone else to have the headache of setting up a new service.'

He grinned. 'Bingo! We could be a good team.' He

caressed the controls and adjusted the flaps on the wing. 'You ready? We're going in.'

The noise of the plane engine changed and the little cabin tilted as they began their circling descent to what he hoped would become her new home.

## CHAPTER SEVEN

Dawn squirmed against her mother as her ears blocked from the altitude change. Montana slipped her little finger into her daughter's mouth so she would suck and swallow and pop her ears.

As a diversion from the risks of landing small aircraft, Montana mulled over what Andy had said. He seemed a little obsessed with the hospital and the town, and he lived with an older doctor and his housekeeper. Obviously he'd been devastated at the loss of his wife and now devoted himself to his work.

What about friends? Or other women?

Didn't he have a life?

Did he expect she'd be as committed as he was because she'd lost her husband too? Was that why he'd been so keen to have her come?

Maybe he'd planned to staff the hospital with bereaved doctors and nurses. A sound plan, she told herself, tongue in cheek. She had to smile at her fanciful meanderings but they were coming in and the thoughts helped to divert her mind away from the ground looming up at her.

She hadn't guaranteed she'd stay at the lake and she might not feel the same next week. Going on her recent form, she might not feel the same in the next minute. 'I hope this works out as you plan. That Dawn and I can settle here for a while.'

In the few seconds before he answered Montana realised that as the pilot he was responsible for the safety of their descent. What was she thinking? Now was not the smartest time to distract the pilot.

'Please, ignore me and concentrate.' There was a squeak of sheer terror in her voice and he looked across at her and smiled reassuringly.

'I've done this hundreds of times.'

She grimaced at him. 'Why does that not reassure me? You only have to blow it once in a plane.' She'd tried for lightness and she wasn't sure she'd pulled it off, but he returned to her previous statement and his relaxed example helped her hands unclench.

'I know there are no guarantees you'll love the lake like I do,' he said. 'That's understandable. We'll see what the next few weeks bring.'

They landed smoothly and taxied up to park near a tin shed that proclaimed a welcome to the great state of Queensland and to Lyrebird Lake, and Montana thought how she would have felt welcome anywhere that had firm earth beneath her feet.

As they waited for the propeller to stop revolving, Andy slid his hands onto his thighs, which drew her eyes to that strongly muscled part of him, and when she realised she was staring she whipped her gaze away. He turned to grin at her. 'Well, you survived your flight and here we are.'

Indeed. Was it hot in here? 'Thank you for getting us here safely.' Her comment was hopefully distracting from her red cheeks. 'Interesting airport.' She looked around at the deserted tarmac, though there did seem to be some activity in a hangar across the grass.

Andy followed her gaze. 'There're great people in the flying club out here. I'll have to bring you out to one of their barbeques. Always a fun evening under the stars with a bunch of larrikins.' He inclined his head towards the hangar. 'Though they do take their flying seriously and I can't beat one of them in the flour bombing contests.'

Montana blinked. 'The what?'

Andy laughed. 'Sorry. It's a competitive sport. You open a window in the cockpit while flying over a target site. Then drop a bag filled with household flour out the window. The person who's bomb lands nearest the target, wins!'

She spread her hands. And?

He laughed and the sound made her smile. 'Mine gets snatched out of my hand when I try and misses by a mile.'

Now she knew. Random.

The propeller swung on its last rotation and Andy flicked the last of his switches and then climbed out to come around to her side.

He opened her door and warm air rushed in and wrapped around her like welcoming arms. She hoped it was prophetic. She hadn't expected to feel embraced by the new town, but the warmth and the sounds of birds and swishing of wind in the trees all felt exciting.

Andy reached in to undo the strap around Dawn and Montana's seat belt, and the release of the restraint made her feel suddenly lighter, almost symbolic of her new life.

'Here,' Andy said. 'Give me Dawn while you climb out.'

Dawn whimpered when she was lifted but settled happily on Andy's shoulder. Montana was reminded how at ease he was with her daughter. Maybe he was like that with all babies and she was being too personal here.

He extended his other hand to help steady her as Montana climbed awkwardly over the doorframe, but soon her feet were thankfully on the earth again. 'Would you think I was silly if I bent down and kissed the ground?' A joke. But she really wanted to.

His green eyes sparkled with mischief and she had the sneaking suspicion he knew what she'd been thinking.

'This way,' he said. 'My car is in the shed and it's too hot to leave you both out in the sun while I get it. We'll walk across and I'll drive it back to the plane for the gear.'

He shifted Dawn down his chest so he could cover her head from the sun and the glare, and she loved the way he did these little things so naturally.

Duncan would have handled having a baby in his life twenty-four hours well, too, she reminded herself swiftly. Just to ground herself in that reality.

Surreptitiously she watched Andy stride across the grass beside her and she strained to hear his one-sided conversation with Dawn.

'You're a big girl now, Dawn. Did you enjoy your first flight? You were very brave. You must be Mummy's daughter because she's very brave. You are going to love it here.'

I hope we are, Montana thought, because she had the feeling that Andy would do everything in his power to look after them and help them settle. Perhaps it was the euphoria of being on solid earth again, but she couldn't help a warm surge of emotional certainty that this was the start of something big. This opportunity of fresh beginnings, here in Lyrebird Lake with its not-an-airport airport.

As they drove through the town, Montana's burgeoning confidence expanded. The main street, wide, and with huge shady trees planted in the middle of the road felt welcoming.

People waved at Andy as he drove by and the whole

atmosphere was one of enjoyment of life. The buildings were old but restored in heritage greys and blues and she smiled across at the man who was obviously proud of his town.

'You look happy to be home.'

'I am. Hopefully you'll feel the same, soon.'

Me too, she thought. She settled for saying, 'Thank you.'

# *Montana*

## CHAPTER EIGHT

L ike the flight, settling into Lyrebird Lake proved much easier than she'd anticipated, and Andy was only one of the people who made it so.

The house was large, sprawling from a business end to a living end, with the rear of the house holding the kitchen and lounge areas. All the bedrooms opened onto the verandas and were each side of a long hallway. Montana's room was large, high-ceilinged and had double doors out to the veranda. Oodles of room for a cot, though an old fashioned hospital baby bassinet with wheels had been waiting for her, made with fresh white hospital sheets and a pink hand-knitted quilt that felt so soft and warm.

Two empty rooms lay between her and Andy up the hall-way, one between her and Louisa, and Ned was opposite Andy.

Ned, while supposedly a semi-retired GP, was a white-browed, hyperactive Scotsman who bounced from one task to another with boundless energy and constant discussion.

He ran a clinic every afternoon in a rundown set of consulting rooms at the front of the house, played chess on

Tuesdays and Thursdays and was the local Rotary Club president. For fun he carved native animals out of driftwood, while he chatted, and the house was bedecked with his figurines. Sadly, he found it harder with his deteriorating eyesight to instil fine detail in his carvings and mentioned that often.

He hobbled a little with his stiff hip, and if he misplaced his glasses — which he did frequently even in that first twenty-four hours Montana was there — he could barely read the brand name on a cereal pack, but she had the impression his diagnostic skills were in no way diminished by his eyesight.

Intuitive and caring, Ned saw through Montana's facade of calmness on the first day and she found herself sharing more with him about her loss of Duncan and her struggle to move on from it than she had with either of her girlfriends or Andy.

She'd felt lighter, after their talk, and wondered if Ned had been as restorative with Andy. Maybe Ned was the lyrebird, the one that brought healing, which he just had to tell her about in one of his rambling discussions.

Ned's housekeeper, Louisa, was a round Yorkshire dumpling of a woman with merry eyes and big breasts whom Dawn cuddled into like a pillow from the first moment.

The feeling of comfort appeared mutual as Louisa had commandeered Dawn and whisked her off to the kitchen to watch while she cooked.

The first morning Montana came in to breakfast, after a disturbed night with her daughter, Andy welcomed her with a smile and a cup of tea.

Louisa waved from over at the stove.

He looked very pleased with himself as he handed her the

cup. 'Your jasmine tea, *madame*. Perhaps I could cuddle Dawn?' He tilted his head. 'If that's okay with you?'

Dawn had been upset overnight, no doubt picking up her mother's unsettled mood, and she guessed Andy must have heard her.

Her stomach dropped. 'Did she keep you awake?' And everyone else?

Andy's forehead crinkled. 'No. I only heard her for a couple of minutes all night, so you must be an awesome mother.' He looked so sincere that Montana relaxed.

She'd thought the walls were solid wood. Still, it was weird to suddenly share a home with people she barely knew, and she couldn't help worrying that her new baby would disrupt the household.

Andy had his hands out so she passed Dawn to him and sat down. Now her daughter semi-grimaced at Andy as if delighted to be handed over.

'Typical. That's the first smile I've seen. She likes you alright.'

'What have you done to your poor mother, missy?' Andy admonished Dawn with a teasing finger. Then he glanced across as if to assess Montana's fatigue. 'You should take it easy today,' he said. 'If you're up to it, we'll go for a walk along the lake this evening, show you the lie of the land. Otherwise you should be sleeping when Dawn sleeps.'

She raised her brows at him. 'Who's the mother here? It's strange to have someone say something to me that I'm always telling other new mums to do. I find it's hard to do it myself.'

'Funny that,' he said with a lopsided grin. 'Ned is always telling me to take more time off.'

And he obviously wasn't, if his holiday had been the first in three years.

When Andy went off to the hospital the house seemed to

echo with his absence, although Ned and Louisa made sure she had company if she wanted it, along with further encouragement to rest when she needed.

By that evening, Montana found herself glancing at the clock to check the time more often than usual, until she realised she'd begun to calculate the time until Andy returned. She did notice a little skip in her heart rate when he walked in. Surely because she had more time than she'd expected on her hands.

He made her sit up, and engage, with his easy smile and laughing green eyes when he asked about her day. She couldn't help her own smile in return. She glanced across at Louisa and Ned, who were heads together discussing something about fetes, and seemed to have faded into the distance since his arrival. They weren't paying attention to her and Andy.

'I feel unproductive,' she offered. 'I haven't achieved anything. *They* won't let me help.'

He glanced at the older couple, laughing as they peeled vegetables and conversed together. 'No discontent there, business as usual. I believe *your* instructions were to rest.'

'That I managed in spades. And I do feel lazy.'

'Come for that walk I mentioned this morning then. Before tea.'

A walk in the cool of the evening did sound heavenly, Montana thought, and no doubt Dawn would enjoy an outing in the fancy old pram Ned had produced with glee this afternoon.

But surely Andy didn't need to go out again. 'Don't you

ever sit down? You've just come in.' Selfish woman, she admonished herself.

Andy shook his head. 'I'd enjoy it, too. I relax better upright. If it includes a walk, even better.'

After some organising of the pram and its precious cargo, the three of them meandered along the lakeside path under overhanging trees, and the cool evening breeze was as delightful as Montana had imagined it would be.

Still, two people out together with one baby almost felt like a family excursion and Montana was conscious not to lean too close towards Andy as they walked. She didn't want anyone they encountered to get the wrong idea about their relationship.

The houses they passed all seemed to be built of heavy timber and pretty gables. The fronts faced the lake.

If this was suburbia then Montana hadn't seen anywhere like it as peaceful or pretty, and the evening seemed to wrap the three of them in hazy contentment.

She felt like a child peering through other people's windows at Christmas, which was strange when in Coffs Harbour she had her own house and garden. Suddenly home felt a million miles away from here and not a quarter as attractive.

'Do you ever think of buying a house around here?' The words fell out and she hoped they weren't too personal, but Andy didn't seem worried she'd asked.

'I might do some time in the future.' He smiled across at her. 'I did buy my dream block of land at the end of the lake, but most of my time is spent at the hospital or on home visits, so I don't need to build a house of my own just yet.'

He waved his hand back towards the hospital. 'At the moment I wouldn't be able to give a house and garden the care they needed until more medical relief arrives.'

Montana wondered if that was really true, or did Andy choose to spend so much time finding things to do so he didn't have to be alone in a house of his own. Stop it.

None of her business why Andy doesn't have a home. Too personal.

They meandered on and the sun set behind the hills as they turned back towards the doctors' house.

The three weeks left in January passed in a blur, with what became ritual walks along the lake in the evening and caring for Dawn through the day.

Late in the month Andy took Montana to the flying club for a barbeque and she followed him nervously out of the car.

Andy was greeted like a long-lost friend and he introduced Montana to Paul, the local flying instructor.

'Do you fancy learning to fly, Montana?' Paul asked with sweep of his hand towards the sky.

'Not at the moment, thanks,' she said, and glanced across at Andy whose laughter-filled eyes dared her to tell Paul what she really thought.

'You'll have to come up with me one day,' Paul said, oblivious to the shudder from Montana. 'Andy's only an amateur in a baby plane.'

He pointed to a petite brunette serving salad at the trestle table. 'My wife has a beautiful biplane, a Tiger Moth. Now, that's real flying.'

Driving home later, Andy teased her about her not taking up Paul's offer.

'I can just see you with goggles and a flying jacket in the front of the Tiger Moth.'

'Not.' Montana refused to take the bait. 'But thanks for

taking me out. It was lovely to have a change of scenery and, you're right, the flying club mob are larrikins but lovely ones.'

Montana had begun to itch for some work, an occasional relief shift even at the hospital when Andy told her about a staff member off sick, but Andy insisted Montana relax and enjoy Dawn while she settled into motherhood.

It was like stolen time and Montana had never done so little for so long. Despite some occasional homesickness for her friends, she felt more at peace than she had since Duncan had died.

She realised the gnawing pain from her loss of Duncan had been eased by her love for Dawn and the warmth from her new housemates. And she could say she was beginning to feel like she belonged at the lake.

February saw Montana drift to the surgery end of the house and glance over the list of patients. At least she could see if there were any nursing tasks she could do for Ned, like occasional dressings or injections or even minor suturing.

She began to spend an hour or so in the surgery but as the days passed more clients began to be allocated to her time slot. Soon her hour had stretched to two.

Montana discussed with Ned the need for a well-women's clinic and the idea to use her women's health certificate for the first time in years gave her the incentive to scan the internet for health sites to update her knowledge.

One morning she realised she'd been there six weeks already and Andy seemed to have fallen into a routine of including her in his day.

He arrived in the kitchen and swooped on Dawn who lay propped up as she stared fascinated at the world from her pram while Montana ate her breakfast.

'Would you like to come for a turn around the garden, gorgeous,' he asked, 'before I sit down for my breakfast?'

Dawn's little face lit up as soon as Andy entered her vision and she had even begun to coo when he picked her up. Montana realised that she wasn't the only person falling under Andy's spell. Dawn adored him.

Her own relationship with Andy hadn't changed since she'd moved into this house, but she wished she could say the same about the way she reacted to him emotionally.

To Montana he was unfailingly polite and supportive and she had to admit she looked forward to seeing him in the mornings and evenings, but there was still a certain reserve between them that wasn't there for Dawn or the others.

But, then, he was everyone's favourite.

He teased Louisa indulgently, and the affection in the scoldings she gave him showed how much she enjoyed their exchanges. Ned treated Andy like one of his favourite nephews. Apparently, Ned had a son but despite Montana's gentle inquiries nobody enlarged on his whereabouts.

Apart from breakfast and their evening walks, Montana saw very little of the workaholic Andy in the intervening hours.

As she watched Andy bear Dawn away, Montana worried over her growing feelings for the man. To her dismay, he appeared in her thoughts far too often, and snippets of new memories would drift her into a reverie when she least expected it. She suspected her panicked misgivings during the plane trip may have substance. Following Andy out here could be detrimental to her peace of mind.

Then there was the fair lashing of guilt over her faithlessness to Duncan.

Both Andy and Ned treated her like a princess, opened doors, pulled out her chair, stood when she entered the room. It was totally different from her life with Duncan, who had loved her but had expected almost the opposite. Duncan had been the prince, the doctor and the artist, and she the person responsible for the mundane tasks of day-to-day living as well as all nurturing and household business.

Here Louisa managed the house, Andy the hospital and Ned the clinic. Montana looked after Dawn and learnt about Lyrebird Lake.

She knew Andy suspected she still missed the day-to-day interaction from her husband — or maybe that was what he had missed the most when his wife had died — but she wished he wouldn't try to replace that because she found it harder to picture Duncan's face each day and easier to conjure up Andy's.

She didn't feel comfortable losing the memory of her husband so quickly and easily, and the rising tide of guilt was the only tarnish on her peaceful life.

What she could see even without actually spending much time with Andy was how much the town relied on him. Ned couldn't suture and had difficulty when he tried to read the names on drug ampoules and bottles because of his diminishing eyesight. Andy slipped those tasks into his already busy schedule and Montana continued to take on what tasks she could to lighten his load.

Andy dealt with all the hospital admissions and transfers to the base hospital, minor surgery and emergencies, and apparently worked on the disaster rescue team when needed.

How did he have time for sleep? She could help somewhere, surely.

Late in the eighth week of her stay Montana swung gently on the veranda swing with the warmth and weight of Dawn on her chest, and watched the sun set over the lake.

She'd have to go in soon for tea, but for the moment the gentle breeze and the reflection of trees in the water were glorious. She felt more energised than she had since Dawn's birth. The days had begun to drag and she realised she was ready to return at least to part-time work.

The noise of the latch on the screen door behind heralded the end of her solitude and she glanced up from the water.

'Hope I'm not intruding.' Andy raised his brows as if she only had to say and he would go again.

Andy really was the most thoughtful man and she didn't understand why he hadn't remarried and surrounded himself with a brood of auburn-haired children when he was so wonderful with Dawn.

Dawn gurgled and wriggled in her arms. Of course, her daughter seemed as pleased as Montana that he'd joined them. She cooed and smiled at Andy's familiar face and Montana thought at least Dawn would know a little of what a father figure was like when she could have so easily have been devoid of all male company. Certainly at Coffs Harbour her daughter would have been in a predominately female environment and her mother wouldn't have been seeking out male company.

Montana patted the seat beside her. 'Join me. We seem to have very little time to chat. Was there something particular you wanted to discuss with me?'

She edged over to make room for him on the swing and Andy's woodsy cologne, which reminded her of the bottle-brush foliage she'd arranged in the vase today, made her realise she'd begun to respond to lots of things that reminded her of Andy. When had that happened?

His was nothing like the expensive cologne Duncan had preferred but was just as manly — Andy's cologne made her think of unobtrusive strength — which was as comforting as the man it belonged to.

# *Andy*

## CHAPTER NINE

Andy savoured the warmth of Montana near him and he acknowledged how much he missed the little feminine aspects of a wife. Montana abounded in those aspects. She dazzled him as she sat here as bright as the sun reflecting off the lake and yet blissfully unaware how much he delighted in her company.

He'd been watching her for a while from the lounge and she'd looked so peaceful he'd been reluctant to break into her thoughts.

'I was wondering...' He paused, still unsure whether to broach the subject. Whether to disturb her peace of mind.

'Wondering what?' she prompted.

Through narrowed eyes, Andy studied the lake. Easier than the punch of looking into her face. 'Wondering if you are feeling settled here?'

'Unless you're planning to evict me, I have no thoughts of moving on. Why do you ask?'

He couldn't help but smile at her response. Evict her? No chance. 'Fancy a bit of work?'

Her chin went up and her smile matched the sparkle in her eyes. 'I was just thinking that.'

Good. He had suspected she might be ready for more than the few hours helping Ned but he hadn't wanted to push her too quickly. 'There are a couple of things I want to run by you.'

She turned towards him and regrettably it became harder for Andy to concentrate with her grey velvet eyes on his so expectantly.

He regathered his wits. 'Ned mentioned your well-women's clinic idea. I think that would be great. We could do it when one of us isn't here to give you the other consulting room. Maybe we could run it a couple of hours one morning or afternoon a week? Louisa said if that was the case, Dawn probably wouldn't mind time with her.' They both smiled. Dawn loved Louisa. And vice versa.

'That sounds excellent.'

She looked happy with that, Andy decided, pleased. He hoped she'd be as interested in his next proposal. 'The other thing is that one of my younger patients, Emma, is pregnant and due in July. I wondered how you'd feel about chatting to her about labour and birth over the next few weeks or months?'

'Of course!' Montana sat up straighter and Andy smiled at her obvious delight. 'How old is Emma?' she asked.

'She's sixteen and about twenty weeks gestation. Her age is a concern, yes, but it isn't my main unease. Physically young women are designed to birth.' He frowned as he thought of Emma and the lacklustre person she'd become in so short a time. 'My concern is that she's changed from an outgoing girl to retreating from everyone. Surly even. Of course a teen pregnancy is a huge event but it's not like her to withdraw. I know the family well and I'm worried about her.

She and Tommy have been close for years, and I think in love since early high school. I'm pretty sure, from what Emma said in very low mumbles, this was their first time and horribly bad luck the contraception didn't work.'

'There but for the grace of the universe would many young first-timers go.' Montana's fine brows drew together and he wanted to follow the movement with his fingers and trace them straight again, but this was too important to be side-tracked by odd fancies.

'You think she's depressed with the unfairness of it, do you mean?' she asked.

He concentrated on Emma. Not on Montana's face. 'Yes. I think there's a risk she could become seriously depressed, especially as her mother seems to be going through a low period at the moment.'

'Her mother's unwell?'

The malady of Clare, Emma's mother, still puzzled him. 'I'd like to think with a bit of positive input from you, Emma will turn back into herself before she gets used to being miserable. I'd hate to think she was still in such low spirits when the baby is born. It could easily lead to postnatal depression and attachment issues. She's so young.'

Montana raised her eyebrows. 'If she is old enough to become pregnant then she's no child. She's a woman. Make no mistake about that.'

He could see the midwife champion coming out in her and he knew he'd been right in thinking she would be good for Emma. 'Of course.'

'That's my own opinion and Emma's lucky she has you to look out for her. Though if she's only halfway there, she may not want to know about labour and the birth process just yet,' Montana added thoughtfully. Her brows were still drawn tight together and he could follow the emotions running across her face as she tried and discarded thoughts and ideas. That lively face reflecting her equally lively thought processes captivated him.

'Why's that?' he asked, wanting to keep her talking so he could watch and enjoy.

'Labour is the last thing a young woman wants to hear about when she's still dealing with the shock of being fertile.'

'Woman's intuition?' He was happy to learn. 'What do you suggest?'

She pursed her lips and he was distracted again as she went on. 'Maybe some sessions on pregnancy health and life-style choices? We still have time to engage her for the benefit of baby and her own health. And that information is not so scary.'

His brain stalled again and he had to blink several times to get his head back together. He kept seeing Montana's mouth and that frozen moment had stunned him silly. He didn't want to go there — or he did and he knew he couldn't — and needed to concentrate on what she was saying.

'I'm sorry.' He blinked again. 'So, you'd be happy to do a couple of sessions with Emma?'

Thankfully Montana seemed oblivious to his mental aberrations and he was glad about that. Very glad.

'Absolutely,' she said. 'It might help to ease her into the idea of learning about her body as we go along.'

He felt sixteen. Everything had double meanings at the moment. He fancied a body lesson — specifically concerning the one beside him — and every day brought more observations for him to store in his expanding folder of what attracted him to this woman.

The mystery and unexpected fascination had started that first day on the mountain. At least he'd figured out what had been wrong with him a month or so ago when he'd drawn that line in their relationship, but every day he struggled more to keep his toes behind the line. 'So you're interested in helping Emma?'

Damn. He'd already asked her that.

'Yes.' She looked at him narrowly, as if to check he was still present or whether he'd clocked out.

'I wanted to be sure,' he said, 'that you're sure.'

'I am.' Two short syllables, packed with conviction.

Andy exhaled. And decided not to speak again until he'd got his brain under control.

'So how did her parents react to the news?' Montana asked after a few quiet seconds' consideration.

He thought ruefully of the intense week he'd had with both sets of grandparents-to-be. 'Moments of unusual interest, but they're coming around. It's even more tricky because Emma's mother isn't well.'

Montana tilted her head. 'In what way, unwell?'

Maybe it would help to clarify his thoughts if he ran it by Montana. 'I wish I knew. Clare still puzzles me but there's something niggling below the surface. She had a car accident a month ago and is complaining of being vague, clumsy and irritable, which is unlike her. There's nothing on her cerebral CT scan, and I'm not sure, but I think I'm closer to working it out.'

'Hmm. More worry for poor Emma. You need your mum at times like this.' She pondered that a moment longer. 'And the baby's father? Is he into relationships?'

'Her boyfriend, Tommy, agrees on keeping the baby if that's what you mean.' He grinned a little at scatterbrained Tommy being a father. No doubt he'd mature eventually. 'I think he plans to stay around, but he's only eighteen. They've been together for three years.'

'You'll be up for a dads class then?' she asked, a sparkly of mischief in her eyes.

Lord help him, he hadn't seen himself doing that. 'I don't know anything about being a dad!'

'Neither would he, so you can both learn as you go along. I could lend you Dawn for an hour for show and tell. You're pretty good with her.'

She was teasing him and he decided he quite liked it, but he wasn't pretending to know something he didn't. 'I'll help but you have to come with Dawn.'

'The value will be in the guy aspect. But early days. We can talk about that later.'

Her face her whole body radiated excitement and it was infectious. Despite his muddled thoughts, his mood had lifted with hers. 'It's not too much work for you to start with? The clinic *and* Emma?'

She shook her head vehemently. 'Oh no, not at all. I'd love to help with both. To be honest, I'm starting to climb the walls here without a project to work on.'

'Boredom can be good.' He smiled at her dubious expression. 'Seriously though, that's wonderful. I'll set Emma up for later this week or early next week and talk to Ned about the clinics.'

A week later Montana watched out of the lounge room window as Andy's car pulled into the drive.

A too-thin blonde girl — young woman, she corrected herself — had her head down and didn't look up at the house when Andy opened the passenger door.

So, he opened doors for everyone. It was such a lovely gesture, and to see him doing this for young patients like

Emma, as well as older adults, made her appreciate him even more. Although, she realised belatedly, it may have been because Emma didn't want to get out of the car.

Watching the teenager drag her reluctant feet toward the house, Montana sighed. She glanced at the table and chairs she'd set up with pamphlets and a baby bonus gift pack Misty had sent up from New South Wales. It wasn't so much a statement about learning, as information Emma could take away when she left and maybe read at home.

Montana aimed for the whole session to illustrate the fact that a mother's choices affected a baby's future, but none of it mattered if she couldn't engage Emma's interest.

Montana twitched a tablecloth over the table to create a bumpy but blank face to the room. Hiding the books and bundle. She'd see if curiosity would encourage Emma's interest later.

Montana moved to the door as Andy ushered in the girl. His face showed palpable relief when he saw her. 'Here's Montana. Montana, this is Emma.'

He looked handsome this morning in his open-necked shirt, and his thick hair was tousled as if they'd had the windows open on the drive. Or he'd been running his hands through it repeatedly. His stressed relief at seeing Montana made her realise for the first time that he wasn't always as comfortable with everybody as he was with her. Which only warmed her to him even more.

'Hello, Emma,' she said with a welcoming smile. 'Thank you, Andy. We'll sit on the lounge, not at the table, and just chat for a bit.'

Andy tapped the ends of his fingers together a few times perhaps to prevent raking them through his hair again and looked hopelessly out of his depth. He stepped back. 'Do you need me?'

Montana took pity on his discomfort and shook her head, although Emma threw him an anguished glance. 'That's fine. How about if you run Emma home later when we're finished, unless you get called away?'

'Great idea. I'll leave you ladies to it then, and be back in a little while?'

He dropped the keys onto the bookshelf as if they were hot. 'Emma can give directions if I'm not around and I'll use the utility if I need to go to the hospital.' Andy waved and backed out of the room. Both women watched him go.

'Well, you really had him scared,' Montana commented, and watched the sudden glint of amusement in Emma's face before she schooled her features into a surly frown again.

Gotcha, Montana thought with an inner smile and a little relief.

She watched Emma perch uncomfortably on the edge of the lounge and share her glances between the door and the floor, and tried to remember how it had felt at sixteen in the headmaster's office. She really hoped Emma wasn't thinking like that.

Montana smiled. 'I gather you're a bit nervous about being here?'

'Andy said I had to come.' Emma darted a quick look at Montana and narrowed her eyes. 'I'm keeping my baby.'

Ah, so this was the issue.

Fair enough then. Montana could understand her attitude. 'Great. Did Dr Buchanan mention that I'm a midwife? I'm a good person to know because I catch babies.'

Emma smiled reluctantly.

Montana went on. 'But your baby isn't going to be here for a long time and Dr Buchanan and I thought you might like some extra knowledge to help you through your pregnancy.'

Montana paused, didn't rush to fill the silence, and

waited. The silence lengthened. The relaxed expression on Montana's face didn't change, but Emma began to fidget and finally she looked at Montana.

Emma looked around avoiding Montana's face. 'What are you going to talk about?'

'I guess I need you to participate and ask questions, otherwise you won't take home as much as you could have. It would help if I knew what you would like to know.'

Emma scanned the room again, but behind the nonchalance Montana saw a frightened girl.

'Maybe we should get to know each other before I do all the talking,' Montana suggested. She waited, and Emma eventually nodded. 'You could tell me one thing about yourself, Emma. Something about your family, perhaps?'

Emma stayed balanced on the edge of the lounge with her arms crossed but she did answer eventually. 'There's my dad, who has a sawmill. I get on well with him.' She looked down darkly at the carpet. 'Or I did before I was pregnant.'

Life wouldn't be fun for Emma at this moment, Montana could see that, and she softened her tone. 'He'll come around. He's probably trying to adjust the dreams he had — parents have huge dreams in their minds for their children — and now he has to change those pictures into the ones that you will make for yourself.'

Emma looked up and pondered Montana's words before she nodded. This time she met Montana's eyes. 'That does make sense. Thank you.'

That was when Montana saw the first glimpses of the girl Andy had spoken of with such admiration. Encouraged, she pushed on. 'Have you any brothers or sisters?'

'Three older brothers who wanted to beat up poor Tommy.' Emma looked up and her chin tilted. 'But I wouldn't let them.'

Montana liked her more every second. 'I have an idea you could be a pretty strong-minded young woman when you want to be.'

Emma rolled her eyes. 'Men are so dumb sometimes.' She shook her head in disgust. 'As if thumping Tommy would help. Tommy's the only one who understands.'

Montana bit back a smile. 'Well, that's a good thing. Lots of younger men wouldn't be able to get their head around being a father.'

Emma even went so far as to grin then. 'I don't think he's even thought of that, just that it's happened, and we are the ones who have to make the best of it.'

'And your mum?' Montana hoped Emma didn't mind her asking.

'Mum's been sick lately.' Emma frowned. 'I am sorry she's had this worry as well, but if she'd tried to get better, and not be so down, I wouldn't have been away from the house so much and this might not have happened.'

Montana left that statement to lie where it fell, gave it a few moments to settle, and moved the conversation around to why they were there.

'Thank you. That helps me know you a little. I'll add a little about myself and why I think I can help you.' She paused, smiled softly. 'I really do know about having babies because that's my job. As a midwife, I help women when they have their baby in a hospital and support the mum and baby as they learn to breastfeed and get used to each other. Share knowledge in antenatal classes and, as it happens, I do have a brand new baby of my own.'

Emma looked interested at the mention of Dawn. Montana went on. 'I thought we'd talk about pregnancy so you could be comfortable with what will go on in your body as it changes.'

Emma looked out from under her lowered brows. 'You're not going to try and talk me into not having the baby?'

Montana's gaze locked with the girl's and she shook her head emphatically. 'No. That's your decision, Emma, and it seems to me that you are pretty sure what you want to happen. But with that decision comes a responsibility that you do the best for your own health and that of the baby inside you. Is that how you feel?'

She shrugged. A teen's gesture of uncertainty rather than disinterest. 'I suppose so. I know I want my baby to grow healthy, even if it's going to hurt when I have him or her.'

The fear she'd expected was there and Montana nodded. 'One of my jobs is to help you remember women are designed to give birth. You're healthy and young women usually bounce back from birth better than older women, but we might leave that to talk about another time.'

Emma looked relieved.

'Did Dr Buchanan tell you we could have another session if you want later? I think there's way too much to talk about in one day.'

Emma met Montana's look with a sheepish grin. 'He said that. I only came today because he's been so good to me and Tommy, but you're not too bad, so far. I'll probably come back.'

'Thanks,' Montana said, biting back a smile at the faint praise. 'In that case, we'd better get started before I fall out of favour.'

Emma grinned and the tension in the room lessened noticeably.

'Today I thought we'd talk about where you are in your pregnancy now. How many weeks along are you, Emma?'

Emma unfolded her arms and chewed her nail. 'The

ultrasound man at the base said twenty weeks yesterday. I'm halfway there.'

Montana picked up the book of diagrams she had. 'And there he or she is.' She pointed to the twenty-week foetus. 'Your baby is fully-formed and soon you should be able to feel his or her movements.'

Emma craned her neck and studied the picture and Montana gave her the book and reached for another copy of the same publication.

'Did he give you a due date?' Montana flicked forward to the picture of a woman with a full-term baby and showed Emma the page number so she could skip forward if she wanted to.

'Andy says the seventeenth of July.'

Montana nodded. 'Right in the middle of the year. Your best present ever will arrive some time in our Winter, which will be helpful when you are big and heavy for the cooler weather. You'll be having a Christmas in July baby.'

Emma looked up and a faint glimmer of a smile lit her pale face. 'That's the first positive thing anyone has said about my baby.'

Poor Emma. 'That will change. Babies make everyone smile.'

Montana knew now, with relief, Emma would be fine. She was smart, would have family support by the end, and was protective of her baby. 'Everyone else is still in shock, honey. Now that this baby is a reality they'll come around. That's what families and good friends do.'

Emma pursed her lips thoughtfully and nodded then settled more comfortably back into the lounge.

Montana sat back in her own chair. 'Okay. Let's talk about where your baby is up to now.'

Emma met Montana's eyes. 'It's hard to think of it as a

baby. I haven't even got a belly, especially as I threw up so much that I've lost weight.'

Montana nodded. 'For some people that's normal. That should settle around this time. It's the surge of hormones of early pregnancy, and other hormones come more into play now. Just make sure you have something in your stomach before your feet hit the floor if it still bothers you.'

'Like toast. Yuk.' Emma screwed up her face.

'Even a dry biscuit is good enough. A few cracker biscuits or a sweet plain biscuit is fine. If you can't get someone to bring it to you, keep a jar by your bed and eat before your feet hit the floor. It's worth it, believe me.'

Emma stopped chewing her nails. 'How about a pretzel?'

'Nothing wrong with a couple of pretzels, just don't overdo it on the salt. It's better for you than losing your breakfast every day.'

Emma grinned and it changed her whole face. She was engaged and present and very pretty. 'Cool. I'll try it and let you know.'

'Just remember when you're eating properly you need to start thinking about making sure you have all the nutrients and vitamins your baby needs because he/she is greedy to grow and will take all the goodness and leave you nothing if you don't eat enough of what she, or he, needs.'

'She,' Emma said with conviction. 'I think it's a girl.'

Montana smiled as the young woman within began to show herself more consistently. 'Okay, then. I will stick with the feminine pronoun. It's easier than using she/he all the time.'

'How big is it? I mean, she,' Emma corrected herself 'right now?'

'Right now she's a tiny baby. About two to three hundred grams. Say, the size of a big banana. In two weeks she'll put on another one hundred and fifty grams — that's near a pound in the old measurements. She'll grow from around six and a half inches long to about eight inches at twenty-three weeks. That's the size of a small doll.'

Emma's eyes had grown wide and round. Much like a small doll. 'Wow.'

Montana nodded. 'It's pretty impressive. Everything is made in miniature and over the next twenty weeks will double in size, which means her brain is growing really fast. Mothers need to know that what they eat, drink, smoke or expose themselves to are super important.' She thought of examples. 'I wouldn't use pesticides or strong cleaning agents — because toxins and poisons can affect the way a baby's brain grows.'

'I want her to have a brain,' Emma said dryly. 'That's pretty important to keep in mind, as far as I'm concerned.'

'That's what I meant about responsibility. Even a mother's emotions can impact on a baby, so if Mum is always sad then the baby thinks it's normal to be feeling sad a lot of the time. That's why I tried not to be too sad when I was pregnant.'

Emma looked up with a mix of curiosity and ready sympathy. 'Why were you sad?'

'My husband died last year. A sudden brain haemorrhage when I was first pregnant, and now I have a nearly two-month-old daughter called Dawn. So, I'm bringing up my daughter without a daddy.'

Emma sucked in a breath. 'That's so sad for Dawn.'

Montana tried not to think about that, at least not *too* often, but now Emma had put the words out there and Montana had a sudden clear picture of her daughter that morning. Bouncing on Andy's lap while Montana ate, and she realised how often she'd come to the kitchen to retrieve her daughter to find Andy chatting away to her as if she understood every word he said.

Dawn thought she had a father.

It was an unsettling concept, but she needed to concentrate on Emma and think about that curly one later.

'Why did you call her Dawn?' Emma asked.

Montana didn't want to foster any wild ideas so she approached her answer with caution. She wouldn't lie but she would try to steer away from Dawn's place of birth. 'Because she was born right at sunrise.'

'In your hospital?'

'Dawn was born nearly three weeks early and I was a bit too far away from my hospital at the time.'

'Were you at home?' Emma persisted.

Yep. She'd have to tell her. Montana smiled wryly. 'She was born on the side of a mountain.'

'On the side of a mountain?' Emma stared, open-mouthed and horrified. 'Who was with you?'

Oh boy. Montana extended one hand in an I-didn't-plan-it wave. 'Nobody was really with me, although an inquisitive wallaby and her joey watched me, but Dr Buchanan arrived soon after and my baby and I are both fine.'

'That is crazy.' Emma shook her head vehemently. 'I am so *not* having my baby on a mountain.' Emma shuddered and her hand crept up to cup her stomach.

'I didn't mean that to happen. I was going back to town that day. Dawn arrived a bit fast for my plans.'

Emma's brows drew together ferociously. 'If you know so much about giving birth, how come you didn't have your baby in a hospital?'

*Got me there.* Montana shrugged. 'That's how my birth experience panned out, but that's rare. Usually you have plenty of notice, sometimes days or weeks of warnings, before you go into labour. And labour is usually hours and hours long.'

Not quite how she'd choose to explain signs of labour but at least Montana felt she had Emma's attention now. 'Everyone has a different birth, some better or different to others, and we can't really choose which experience we're going to have. We can only learn about the choices available and the sequence of events to prepare. But we'll talk about that another day because it's a long time before you have to think of your baby's birth.'

'Thank goodness for that.' Emma shuddered. 'I'm gonna have a 'sarean.'

'Caesarean.' Montana suppressed a smile. 'Let's talk about that another time as well. You could write questions down as they come to you and we'll cover them when you come back. Okay?'

Emma nodded but she remained a bit wide-eyed. Montana needed to bring her back to the present. 'Let's talk about the pregnancy,' she said briskly. 'What other symptoms have you had, apart from nausea?'

'I cry a lot,' Emma said after a moment's thought. 'But I'm going to try to think of happier things now because I *do not* want my baby to be sad all the time.'

The vehemence in Emma's voice surprised them both and Montana nodded. One good outcome already. Andy would be pleased. Montana was. 'It's different when you think of your baby as real and needing you to mother her even before she's born, isn't it?'

Emma's eyebrows drew together in a scowl. 'How come Tommy gets off so lightly? He doesn't have to worry about anything now until she's born.'

'No. Nothing.' Montana risked a tease. 'Except that your brothers want to kill him!'

'I'm the one who had to fix that, too,' Emma said with a dramatic shrug, and Montana laughed.

An hour later Montana heard Dawn cry and she closed the book and stood up. 'That's it for today, Emma. My baby calls. Come and meet Dawn.'

Emma was already on her feet. 'Yes, please.'

# Andy

## CHAPTER TEN

Andy had Dawn under his arm like a little pink football. She felt incredibly warm and precious tucked against his side. There was something adorable about a baby that gazed up at him with her mother's eyes.

'Mummy is busy at the moment, poppet,' he said. 'She's inside, honest, and you have to come out with me and look at all the trees waving in the breeze.'

She was such a cutie, Andy thought as he swung her up into his other arm and turned towards the water. 'See the big black swans? They look like ships on the lake. Maybe you and me and Mummy could go for a trip in a boat one day. You'd like that.'

Dawn gurgled and pursed her lips and cooed as if trying to impart a secret to him and he grinned down at her. 'You're talking. Yes, you are. Such an advanced little thing at only eight weeks. It must be the company. Your Uncle Andy is always here for you. You just give me a yell and I can come and talk to you.'

He heard the door open behind him and turned to see Montana and Emma had finished.

The warmth in his stomach grew as Montana smiled at them. 'Are you two having a nice time?'

'We sure are.' He beckoned to Emma. 'Come and meet this little cutie, Emma.'

Emma edged across shyly and stroked Dawn's little foot. 'She's so tiny.'

Montana laughed. 'She's big now. Your baby will be even tinier.'

Andy smiled at Emma. 'Did you have a good morning?'

'You bet,' Emma said, and he could see the difference in her already. She clutched a bag of reading material and wore a full-sized grin. Montana had the magic all right, but he'd known that.

He watched Montana studying Emma and the glow in his chest came back as if someone had poked at a fire with a stick and blown on it.

He looked away to the girl. 'Have you decided when you're coming back, Emma?'

Emma looked from Montana to Andy and back to see if she had it correct. 'This time next week, if that's okay? Montana said she'd talk to my year advisor at school and we'll do a child studies project as we go along. That will help with my marks when I have to leave school in the middle of the year.'

'Great idea. I'll run you home, then, if you're ready.' Andy held out his hand and Montana handed him the car keys and he offered her Dawn. 'Why don't you come with us, Montana? We could drive around the lake on the way home.'

His hand dropped as Dawn was transferred but he could still feel her mother's warmth on his fingers. Touching her felt as good as he'd known it would and just as dangerous. 'I've seen Louisa and she said she'll keep lunch for us.'

Montana smiled. 'I'd like that.'

His chest expanded as he stood back to allow her to precede them down the steps. Life was good and today was especially delightful. Lucky he'd installed that baby seat in the car. They settled Dawn in the back next to Emma and set off.

After they dropped Emma home, Andy drove the scenic route back in the opposite direction around the lake because he enjoyed the tranquillity — and he was in no rush to lose Montana's company. Strange how each everyday pleasure ramped up when he was with her. The lake seemed clearer, the sky bluer, even the jagged signs of progress in the distant housing development had a certain charm.

'We haven't been out much since you arrived, have we?' He had to admit he'd spent a fair bit of time thinking about where he could take her but hadn't actually made it happen yet. He wondered if she'd even spared him a thought. 'I gather you enjoyed your morning with Emma?'

'I did. Yes. She's great.'

Montana turned her face to his and he could see the enthusiasm there. He knew she had already responded to that magic. He felt his heart rate pick up just with that attention. Imagine if she did more than smile at him — he'd be a basket case.

'I hadn't realised how much I missed interacting with pregnant women,' she said. 'Emma's a sweetie.'

You're a sweetie, he thought. 'I'm glad you like her.'

They drove along, silence companionable rather than awkward between them, through fields that sprouted 'For Sale' signs and passed an early development stage of the future housing estate.

'This will be Lakeside Village when it's finished.' They passed thick stands of gum trees and native shrubs all back-dropped by the lake. 'I think it retains the country feel.'

She turned to give the area a three-sixty and a nod. 'The view is great.'

It was. The estate boasted white kerbs and gutters and houseless cul-de-sacs and he found himself thinking for the first time what it would be like to build a house with a family in mind.

A big house on his land at the end of the lake, with a jetty and a boathouse and a parents' retreat from the hordes of children they'd have. His daydream halted when he realised who he'd been projecting into that role of mother.

Lucky she couldn't read his mind or she'd ask him to pull over so she could get out. So she could run, far and fast.

'Where did you say the new mine site is?' Montana was definitely in a different headspace to him and this was a good thing.

He forced his mind to shelve his future home for later so he could answer her question. 'Twenty kilometres due west. They've put through a straight road so it won't take long to drive between the estate and the mine.'

'When do they open the road?'

'Soon.' He needed to have the hospital ready. 'That's why I'm hoping the hospital will get the upgrade. We're an hour closer than the base hospital and although the mine does have helicopters which would take the serious casualties away, we do want their custom.'

She pondered that. 'When does production start?'

'It's started.' He glanced across at her and then back to the road. He hadn't noticed the way her nose had a faint dusting of freckles on the end.

*Stay on track, idiot.*

He frowned at himself and returned to topic. 'They have a tent city at the moment and the company plans to build the first fifty houses at Lakeside in the next six months.'

'That's a big influx of families for a small town. You should be happy about that.'

That startled him. 'Why wouldn't I be happy?'

She tilted her head and examined his expression. 'You had a fierce look on your face. Almost ferocious.'

'Ferocious?'

He grinned at that observation. At least he wasn't invisible to her. He'd been chastising himself. Hadn't realised so strongly.

'Not the word,' she asked?

'No. I'd be happy. Not just for the town either. It's a godsend for those further out on the land trying to hang onto their properties until the next rain.'

She inclined her head. 'Rain, yes, it would be great if that was more reliable.'

He pondered the stress some of his more distant patients lived under. 'We've quite a contingent from up to two hundred miles west coming in to work at the mine. Those farmers without trades fill positions like mine maintenance or driving trucks. And then there are the extra three hundred skilled workers that will come in when the mine becomes fully productive.'

'Exciting times for Lyrebird Lake.'

He nodded at her observation. 'It is. That spells change not just to the services like the hospital and schools, but the shopping, and of course the pubs will do a roaring trade.'

She nodded sagely. 'More babies for our new maternity unit.'

'I like the way your mind works.' He chuckled. 'We have to talk about that. Have you thought any more about how we could go about setting up a maternity service?

'I am interested if I can get the midwives.'

He sighed with relief and pulled over so he could concentrate on her comments without having to divide his attention. Dawn was asleep so they could talk undisturbed.

He hadn't realised how much he'd dreaded that she mightn't want to stay. That in itself was a concern for his state of mind. 'Do you think you could attract other midwives here as well?'

She considered her answer. 'With caseload I could. It's a big carrot for midwives to be able to care for women in a structured midwifery environment. The idea of a midwifery-run clinic has real appeal there. Nearly every clinic I know has waiting lists of midwives who want to do caseload.'

'I don't have a waitlist.' Far from it, Andy thought.

After several moments' reflection, she continued. 'It's the hospitals that have trouble finding staff to work in areas midwives don't want — under conditions that don't suit them. Caseload is so flexible and rewarding if you have a good team.'

He didn't quite get caseload, knew it was to do with low-risk women usually and consultation with medical care only if needed. But he knew it worked well in other areas. Misty had mentioned it more than once. 'I understand the concept but you'll have to explain the finer points.'

'Sure, but what about you and the main hospital? You won't be able to keep up with just Ned.'

'I know.' He raked a hand through his hair. 'I've put a few feelers out and if I can't get any stayers then I'll just have to pull a few favours and think in short-term appointments until we find someone.'

'You care,' she observed quietly.

He took one hand off the steering wheel where it rested and gestured to the rolling hills in the distance. 'This place has become my home, maybe my passion, and I want to see it work for a lot of reasons.'

'I begin to see why you suggested I come here.'

He turned his head and looked at her. Did she? His lips twitched at the corners. 'Do you?' He wasn't sure he knew in the beginning. It was getting clearer now the more he was in her company. She and Dawn had become essential to him.

He gestured to the grassy-verged picnic spot and turned to face her. 'Do you want to get out and sit at the table for a while? If she wakes, Dawn can lie on the rug and watch the leaves.'

'Sure.' But she appeared deep in thought.

The conversation faltered while they settled themselves and a stirring Dawn to face the lake. The soft breeze felt warm but should be pleasant for the two girls in his life.

Birds swooped and dived into the lake and further out a dinghy with two young boys drifted as they fished, and Andy felt contentment settle like a rug over him.

'All this organising at the hospital.' She watched one of the boys reel in a fish. 'It's a big job to liaise on your own.'

He thought about that and then shook his head. 'I'm not really on my own. The mayor is supportive and happy to mediate with state government for the funding and building upgrades we need.' He ticked them off on his fingers. 'The project officer at the mine is an old school friend and she's promised to push for support from the company for capital works and cheap rent for hospital employees when the houses are built.'

'You've already done a lot of the groundwork, then.'

'I'm stuck a little at the hospital. The current nursing manager is not interested in midwifery and she has enough on her plate with the changes. She's threatened to leave as soon as we find a replacement, but she's not really in a hurry to sever all ties.'

'And you're telling me this because...?'

He grinned again. 'I wondered if you'd be up to that sort of commitment sometime in the future?'

Montana shook her head. 'Not full-time work. Not until Dawn goes to school.'

He wasn't daunted. In fact he was thrilled she was at least thinking that long term. He could certainly work with that. 'What about three days a week and we'd get you a trainee administrative assistant as well so you could still be hands on in the midwifery clinic when it opens?' He watched her consider the pros and cons and his pulse rate picked up again.

'That's more attractive,' she said slowly. 'What about Dawn?'

'We're still a country hospital.' They had flexibility. Could arrange whatever she wanted. 'Louisa is there but we could set up a nursery in your office if you wanted or on the ward. We could look for a young woman to set up a creche for the staff. Or help you as a nanny-come-receptionist.'

# Montana

## CHAPTER ELEVEN

Montana looked at him as he demolished problems like a bulldozer. His green eyes seemed flecked with the forest around them, she thought fancifully, blazed with determination to build up the hospital services and she could only admire his tenacity but he was pushing her.

She'd see even more of him if they worked together. She had to consider that. 'You've put a lot of thought into this.'

'I'll admit I hoped you might be interested. You could bring a lot of benefits to the hospital and the town.'

This statement blew her away for a moment. She didn't think anybody had ever seen such potential in her. It was an odd feeling and one that left her strangely warmed as well as gobsmacked. 'I don't understand why you have such faith in me.'

He shrugged. 'I do have faith in you. Plus, our current nurse manager, Joan, is not enjoying the administrative tasks that are mounting up. She'd flip if I mentioned the caseload midwifery unit as well. You could be the part-time deputy nurse manager she's decided she needs. The hospital needs someone who relishes new challenges.'

Would she relish the challenge of setting up a midwifery model? In all honesty, yes, but that didn't stop her questioning. 'And you think I'm that person?' She watched his face and there was no doubt there. Why? What did he see in her to instil such confidence in her professional ability?

'I would highly recommend you to the board without a qualm.'

What if she let him down? 'You've never asked about my other qualifications.'

'I've seen your resume. You showed me before we left Coffs. You've been a relief hospital supervisor. You were in charge of the unit at Coffs Harbour and instrumental in setting up the free-standing birth centre there. Misty told me you are good at managing people.' He waggled his brows comically. 'I saw that in the week at your house.'

He'd been watching her.

'I know you've got the paperwork and the experience.' He spoke more seriously. 'And now I know you.'

Montana gazed out over the lake and acknowledged she felt more settled here every day. She could feel the friendships and connections binding her to a place she wasn't sure she wanted to be bound to. What about her other world? What about her old friends and her old life?

What about Duncan and Duncan's house in Coffs Harbour? Was she going to sell it? And the last, startling thought — did this proposal excite her disproportionately because it would involve spending more time with Andy and his beloved hospital?

She shied away from that because it involved comparisons to Duncan. The next thing she'd be thinking Andy could replace him. The thought horrified her.

Her husband hadn't even been gone a year and she had these...Feelings. Toward another man.

What sort of woman was she to contemplate such disloyalty to Dawn's father?

'It's a big commitment,' she said finally, twisting her fingers. 'I'm not sure I'm ready for that yet. To tell the truth, part of the attraction here is the lack of commitment required. I'd have to change the way I picture the future. I'd have to think about it seriously and not rush into anything.'

Andy was nodding, but there was that glint of determination in his eye that she was becoming more wary of. 'Fine. Believe me, time's not a problem.'

Why did she not accept what he said as true, she thought with irony? He was one-eyed and too passionate about looking after his town, that's why.

He scooped up Dawn, who had suddenly decided she didn't want to lie on her stomach anymore and went on blithely with her tucked under his arm. 'How about in the morning we take a trip up to the hospital and chat to Joan? She could give you an idea of what's involved in the deputy's job and then you could see how you feel about the idea.'

He'd planned this all. A virtual ambush. She knew it. She picked up the blanket and shook it in preparation to leave. 'That is rushing me, don't you think?'

'Nah.' He flapped his hand and shifted Dawn onto his hip. Her little fists waved around joyfully. 'The next board meeting is five days away.'

'Gee, thanks. A whole five days to decide my future.' But she smiled wryly at his single-mindedness while inside a quiet, growing ball of excitement expanded. She could make this work the professional side. If only the personal side wasn't tying her in knots.

~

The next morning, they left Dawn with Louisa so they could visit the hospital.

Montana winced at the stab of guilt when her daughter cried as they walked out the door. This must be how all working mothers felt, but it didn't help the remorse she seemed to be collecting. Then again Dawn could be crying because Andy had left and not her mother.

'She'll be fine. You know it,' Andy consoled her, but knowing Dawn enjoyed her time with Louisa didn't help. The whole thing made her boobs tingle with emotion and hormones despite leaving Louisa a bottle of expressed breast milk.

'Maybe I'm not ready to go back to work yet.'

'We'll see what you think after this morning, but you know Dawn will be fine with Louisa and that she'll call us if needed.'

That was true, Montana consoled herself. It had been the last thing Louisa had said before they left. Andy's understanding and his promise not to pressure her into an immediate decision also helped. That and the knowledge that the hospital was just a short drive away from her daughter. That would always be a plus to life in Lyrebird Lake.

The administration offices were in the original stone part of the hospital building, not the main part, with wooden sash window-frames painted glossy white. They pulled straight up so you could lean out over the gardens and breathe in the summer scent of gardenias.

The building had high ceilings with broad cornices and the boardroom had a massive old fireplace. It resembled an old bank building with wooden-backed chairs around the big oak table that dominated the room.

Joan's office, tucked away to the side of the boardroom, was jam-packed with old nursing books, black ledgers and a towering filing cabinet that looked older than the woman who waited for them with a frail outstretched hand. Joan Winterboune had to be nudging seventy but the snow-white bun caught tightly on her head pulled the wrinkled folds of her face up nicely so that she looked vaguely oriental in appearance and ten years younger than her probable age.

'So you've managed to get her here finally, Andy.' She took Montana's hand and pumped it with a strength belying her size and what Montana had thought to be fragility. She saw sass in Joan's eyes and immediately reassessed. 'Welcome, welcome to my nightmare. He's been promising I'll meet you for a while now.'

Andy grinned. 'It's not that bad, Joan. You'll scare Montana off.'

'Pshaw,' Joan scoffed. 'Young people aren't scared of anything these days. Especially a challenge. If I was twenty years younger I'd take it on myself but I find changes and bureaucrats exhausting. Still, it's my fault. I dislike e-mail, don't enjoy scanning and the printer is broken.'

Andy shook his head. 'You should have told me your printer is broken. I'll have a new one here this afternoon.'

'You don't need to be running after me, as well as everyone else, Andy,' she said, but Montana could tell Joan was touched by Andy's care.

'You know I don't mind.' Andy changed the subject. 'I thought we'd show Montana what a great little hospital we have with a quick tour. Will you join us?'

'Sounds good, but I'm expecting a call so I'll pass. But you have fun.'

Joan waved them off and they left by a side door to cross the garden and enter into the larger main building.

'You mentioned to Joan a while ago that I might be interested in helping her?' Montana slanted a look at him as they walked side by side to the next building.

He didn't meet her eyes. 'I could have done.'

'Cagey, aren't you?' She stopped and waited for him to stop, too, before narrowing her eyes at him. 'When, pray tell?'

He smiled. 'About a month ago. I was waiting for you to get bored.'

'What faith you have in me, sir.'

'I do, don't I?'

She wondered why that comment hit a nerve under her rib cage but decided it was probably a need for strong tea. Things had been a little hectic that morning and she'd missed out.

They entered by the side door of the emergency department. The area housed an observation ward, two triage bays and a minor operating theatre for small suture jobs and plastering.

The office looked over the half a dozen plastic chairs in the waiting room, two of which were occupied.

Andy gestured with his arm. 'We have facilities to keep three patients in beds here and two in the triage bays if we have to.'

A nurse was undressing a familiar looking man's bandaged arm and Andy paused beside her to check the healing process on the patient.

'You remember Paul, from the flying club? He burnt his arm last Friday at another barbecue and Chrissie's been dressing it every day. Chrissie is our registered nurse on duty. Chrissie, this is Montana — she's the midwife staying with us from down south.'

Paul waved his unbandaged hand. 'You'll have to wait for me to heal before I can take you up,' he said, and Montana nodded sagely. Remembering his offer to take her up in his wife's vintage aircraft, which was not going to happen.

Chrissie smiled. 'Hi there, Montana. I hear you made quite a hit with Emma yesterday.'

Montana smiled at the tall blonde woman. 'Word gets around.'

'Not much misses the bush telegraph around here.' Chrissie put her hand to her ear and pretended to listen. Her hand dropped and she grinned. 'Actually, her father is my cousin.'

Montana smiled back. 'I'll remember that.'

Andy nodded at Paul's arm. 'That's looking a lot better. I reckon your wife could bandage it now. Just come back Monday for a final check, or sooner if you have any worries. Okay?'

'Thanks, Andy. I'll drop a turkey off for Louisa. We're culling at home and she said she'd like one for Ned's party.'

'Thanks. Just don't get germs in your burn, mate.' Andy tapped him in a friendly goodbye before he turned to Chrissie. 'Anybody you worried about in the waiting room, Chrissie?'

She shook her head. 'Not at the moment. Just two for dressings. And Bill said Eva's observations are fine so we'll continue with your plans to send her home after four hours.'

Andy nodded. 'Good. Results?'

'The base hospital rang and confirmed the X-ray shows no skull fractures. She wasn't unconscious for more than a few seconds.'

A male nurse filled out a patient chart at the end of the only occupied bed. Andy crossed to him and Montana followed. 'Bill is our enrolled nurse who doubles as an orderly when we need things moved. He's a jack of all trades and we'd be lost without him.'

Bill, a short, thin man in his forties who could have made weight as a jockey, held out his hand and shook Montana's. 'Andy's just saying that because he wants me to take all the oxygen cylinders into town and get them exchanged. And pick up doughnuts.'

He gestured to the patient and lowered his voice. 'Eva's asleep but she's easily woken.'

Andy nodded and checked the chart before they moved on to tour the main ward.

The ward area was divided into five female and five male beds three with elderly patients in them and two ancillary rooms plus a staff cafeteria just off the kitchen.

'The enrolled nurses here are all medication endorsed and run this end, and the registered nurse on duty comes through from Outpatients and gives any S8 medications when needed. Otherwise the nurses down here are self-sufficient.'

He looked at her, satisfied with the information he'd shared. 'What do you think?'

Montana thought he was like a proud father with the hospital which she found endearing. She still thought he needed a life, though. 'Your baby is very nice,' she deadpanned. 'Now where would the midwifery happen?'

He raised his eyebrows suggestively. 'Nitty-gritty, eh?' He spun on his heel and gestured for her to follow him.

'There's a wing tacked onto the main building. This way. It was offered to me as accommodation but I much preferred to stay with Ned and Louisa.'

He spoke over his shoulder as if he couldn't wait to see what she thought when she got there. 'I thought about offering it to you. Lucky I didn't. I'd have missed out on Dawn and the joy of seeing her changes every day.' He paused as if he was going to add something else but didn't.

There were secrets there and she wondered what else he'd been thinking, but they'd arrived at their destination and Andy flipped out a key on his keyring that opened the door. 'The wing is self-contained and has a couple of big rooms and a heap of small ones,' he said.

The hallway was dusty and needed airing but when Montana pulled up the blinds to lighten the gloom, sunlight flooded in through a row of tall north-facing windows. The wing even had a walled courtyard that clients could use in labour and still have privacy. Excitement grew.

Andy stood in the hallway and watched her indulgently as she crossed back and forth between the rooms, amused when she muttered under her breath and she didn't think he missed any of her thoughts. Montana pushed open doors and pulled blinds and when she'd finished she turned to face him with a smile that felt like it exploded out of her.

'This is a great building. Not too big and not too small. It could be perfect.'

Her excitement was reflected in his eyes. As if he'd hoped she'd feel like this. 'There's nothing structural that needs doing.'

'Except for one area. I would need to add a big bath.'

She saw his frown, recognised it for disagreement, even when he tried to erase it. Ahhh. So he wasn't sure about water births.

'Why do you want a bath?' he asked casually, as if needing to cover for his discomfort.

'Pain relief,' she said sweetly, and changed the subject. Oh yes, she'd been there in her old hospital. Waterbirth was a knee jerk subject for those without experience of it. Just keep saying it's for pain relief until he was converted, and avoid the births.'

'Pain relief?' He said a tad sceptically.

She changed the subject. 'We could caseload easily here and open it only when someone was in labour. That way you wouldn't have staff on duty when they weren't needed and if you had three or four midwives on a roster, there would be no problem manning it for the number of births we'd start off with.'

He was watching her with amusement. 'I love seeing you so enthusiastic.'

'You might get sick of it.'

He shook his head. 'Never.'

She laughed inwardly. She'd see. She probably reminded him of himself when he talked about the hospital.

'As for labour ward equipment, I've had a preliminary discussion with the base hospital,' he said. 'They have leftover equipment from refurbishing they are ready to sell cheap if you want to think about a shopping list, and we have some funding from the ladies' hospital auxiliary.'

'Old equipment?' She wrinkled her nose.

'Not old. Necessary things that's all. We'd have to talk to Carrie, our auxiliary president, but if you produce a proposal that covers most things, I'd be happy to support you to the board and the auxiliary for purchases.'

'That's great, but furnishing is the least of our problems.' Montana spun slowly around again, assessing the rooms. 'It could all happen fairly quickly, the physical part, that is. The government requirements, staffing and the liaison with the base for emergencies would take longer. Say four or five months.'

'In time for Emma?' Andy suggested and they both smiled. He was watching her face and she realised she hadn't felt so positive for a long time. 'I was thinking, before then, you could move your well-women's clinic and perhaps antenatal classes over here.'

Oh my, yes. She loved a challenge. She twirled and extended her arms. 'I love the way you think. I'm very excited, Andy.'

He could probably tell. She felt like grabbing him and kissing him. But she wouldn't. *Good grief.*

That wasn't why he'd brought her here, and she needed to remember that. He'd brought her here to establish this service and broaden the staff skill mix.

'I'm pleased you can see potential,' he said solemnly. 'We'll take it slow.'

She didn't believe him but that was okay. She couldn't wait to get started.

Back at the doctors' residence that evening, Montana slipped out of her room after settling Dawn to sleep. The house was encircled by wide verandas and Montana's room was positioned a few doors along the high-ceilinged central hallway from Andy's.

Despite the close proximity of all their sleeping arrangements, she'd never heard any noises from other parts of the house when the doors were shut or actually even seen the door opened to Andy's room.

Unusually, today Andy's door stood open, and she couldn't help glance in as she passed.

She blinked and looked again. Andy stood in the centre of

a huge wood-panelled room holding a tape of some sort and dressed only in jockey shorts. Acres of strong brown chest seemed to fill Montana's vision and after another quick stunned look Montana swung her head away and quickened her step.

Andy's voice followed her. 'Stop! Montana, wait.'

Montana turned back towards him with her gaze firmly anchored on the high ceiling.

Andy chuckled. 'Come on, Montana, I'm sorry I shocked you, but you've seen guys in their jocks before.'

Montana rolled her eyes. 'Come on Andy. How about if I stand with my door open in my bra and undies and call out to you as you go past?' She put her hands on her hips. 'Please.'

Andy grinned hugely. 'Promises, promises,' he joked. 'Any time.'

She rolled her eyes. Such a guy thing.

'Men!' She resumed her progress down the hall and he came out in all his glory to whisper after her.

'Wait, Montana. Can I have your help for a second, please? Really.' He lowered his voice. 'We're having a surprise birthday for Ned's seventieth and I'd like to buy a kilt and jacket on the internet. I've always been hopeless at estimating clothing sizes so I'm trying to get measurements.'

Andy stood there, six feet plus of gloriously muscled male swinging a tape measure in modest but skintight black cotton underwear that left nothing to the imagination. Suddenly there wasn't enough air in the hallway, maybe not enough in the whole of Lyrebird Lake, and she could feel the heat creep up her neck. And other places, which she was bound to ignore.

Looking at someone couldn't make you faint she knew this, being a medical professional so she must be coming down with something. Her tongue dried against the roof of her mouth and she stared down at her clenched hands. She moistened her lips and forced herself to answer past her dry throat.

It was so dry.

She coughed, the dryness cracked and seized and it felt like she'd swallowed a paperclip. She was definitely coming down with something. 'A kilt and jacket would need to fit well. The hardest thing would be—' she glanced again at Andy, saw the expanse of chest and shoulder she'd have to run the tape measure over and her voice cracked on the final words '—the jacket.'

'I tried to do it myself but it's not working.' A tinge of frustration marked his voice. 'Could you help me out? Ned's been at me to buy a kilt because my ancestors were Scots, too, and I want to surprise him on the night.'

'Clan Buchanan?' She raised her eyebrows in disbelief.

'Of Buchanan Castle. I looked it up on the internet.'

'Right. I'll suspend belief. Don't you want to go to a shop and get fitted? That's what most people do.'

'No way to do that here and I don't have the time to go elsewhere. I could really do with some help.' He held up a printed sheet on a clipboard. 'I've typed all the measurements I need on here.'

Montana chewed her lip and pictured herself running the tape-measure intimately over Andy. The picture was a little too graphic and she blushed again. Avoided his eyes.

Silly, but she couldn't help this panicked feeling that had come out of nowhere. She couldn't do this. She couldn't put her hands on him. 'There must be a seamstress in town who'd be better at this than me. I don't even know where I'm supposed to measure.'

'The local seamstress would let everyone know what I'm doing and I want it to be a surprise.'

'What about Louisa?'

'I want to surprise Louisa, too. Please, Montana.' He held his arms wide in a demonstrable plea that only served to draw attention to his sculpted chest and her heightened state of awareness. 'Can't you help a friend in need?'

*Andy*

## CHAPTER TWELVE

He'd been blind. Montana was embarrassed. Her reluctance to accept the tape measure, the way she sucked in a breath and avoided his eyes they all pointed to her discomfit with his state of undress. And perhaps something else?

*Did she think he had a good bod?*

He had a sudden urge to hug her... And tease her. But that would be mean. He had to bite his lip to stop the smile, but he couldn't help winking at her like a mischievous six-year-old. He had no doubt the emotion that shone out of his eyes was the wicked green of unholy amusement.

Her gaze jerked to the thin white tape held between tremulous fingers. Her breathing sounded equally shaky and she narrowed her eyes as if psyching herself up for something she definitely wasn't comfortable with. It reminded him of when she'd climbed into his plane.

He planted his feet. Spread his arms. Tilted his head with a slight note of challenge.

*Come on, Montana. I'm not going anywhere. You can do this.*

She lifted her chin and moved closer. 'Let's get it over with then.'

Andy stood tall and spoke to the top of her head. 'Mean. I wouldn't like you to be too thrilled at the prospect of measuring my manly stature.'

'I'll try not to be.'

She rolled her eyes at him. Darn, she had herself under control now.

'Arm length,' she intoned and then measured inside and out lengths, ignoring the twitch of his skin as he reacted to her touch. 'I'll measure and you write it down.'

He rested the clipboard on top of the old-fashioned table so she could see what was needed and did what he was told between measurements.

'Finally, he does as asked,' she muttered, but there was a hint of playfulness there.

Andy savoured it. Who knew this would turn out so delightfully?

'Wrist.' She measured and waited for Andy to write it down.

The next request made him smile because she was tensing. He actually heard her swallow. 'Biceps.'

His shoulders shook again and when he looked down at her face she'd closed her eyes.

'Do you want it flexed or deflexed?' he said.

She opened her eyes and slanted a look at him. 'You're enjoying this.'

He looked down and grinned. 'I'm having a ball.'

She chewed her lip and he wanted to reach out and say careful of that beautiful mouth, but she was staring at his bicep. Flummoxed? 'I don't know. Flexed, I guess.'

Andy obliged and the tape measure trembled.

Montana changed her mind. 'Um, deflexed, I think.

Otherwise the fabric will be too...' Her voice trailed off and she made a vague gesture with one hand.

'Too... Much?' he supplied helpfully.

Her always contained temper slipped a little. 'For goodness sake, Andy, you're not making this any easier. Get over yourself.'

Good to know she was human.

His chest trembled with suppressed laughter. 'Come on, Montana. This is hilarious.'

To his relief her shoulders slumped and she started to giggle. 'Yes, you're right. I'll try not to stress. I'm having trouble concentrating that's all.' A frown. 'Chest maybe?'

'Follow the prompts on the sheet. We need a shoulder width first.'

She glared at him. 'How about you read it and I'll measure where you tell me?'

His grin widened at the thought. 'That could be fun.'

She looked at the tape in her hand. 'Stop teasing me or I'm out of here.'

He pulled his twitching smile into a serious face and lowered his voice until it was very deep. 'Please, measure the shoulder width.'

She did. Read the numbers for him to write down. 'Done.'

'Neck.'

'Can I pull it tight?' Her voice was sweet even if her intent was not.

He loosened the noose of tape around his neck. 'Play nice. Now the chest.'

To pass the tape around his body she needed to move closer. He could feel her breath against his bare skin, could savour the spread of warmth through his body.

With considerable effort he forced himself to remain

passive. To keep up the light banter. He did not want to scare her off. 'Are you secretly impressed?'

'With your conceit? Yes. Very.' But he was sure there'd been a shake there in the fingers and in her soft exhalation of breath.

'Done,' she mumbled less clearly.

'Waist,' he said, and the laughter was back in his voice. Seriously, how could he not be amused?

She tensed as if to steel herself before circling the tape around his hips and sliding it up to his waist. The feel of her fingers down there required great concentration on his last icy shower.

'Done.'

'From armpit to waist and armpit to hip.' That was easier apparently, or perhaps she was just getting the hang of this measuring gig.

'Inner thigh,' he said in a bored voice but his insides quivered.

She glared at him. 'Do your own.'

He did a dreadful job of the measurement. 'That would be enormous,' he said.

'Like your head. Give it to me. I'm a nurse. I can do this.' She measured with the clinical efficiency of said nurse. 'Done.'

He wrote down the numbers.

'Outside waist to knee.' She had to get down on the floor to measure. He should have felt mean but it was such a lovely viewpoint and the stuff men dreamed off. Fantasy only, he reminded himself. Then he thought, again, about that ice cold shower.

'Width of thigh.'

'It does not ask for that. It's a skirt, for heaven's sake. You are one sicko voyeur.' Eyes sparking, she snatched the sheet to check. And there it was. Andy laughed.

'Kilt, not skirt,' he corrected. 'That's the last one. You want me to move the tackle out of the way?'

'I think you can manage that measurement and the tackle.' She held up both hands in mock surrender. 'No way I'm going near there.'

'Seriously?'

'Yup, I'm done. I've worked up a sweat.'

'And a very nice glow it is.'

They were both teasing, maintaining the breezy banter, but when she looked up at him through her long dark lashes the mood in the room changed subtly. Their eyes met and held, just for a second, before she took a deliberate step back.

Her smile looked a little forced. 'I'm not sure I can remember the last time I actually giggled. You're a menace.'

Despite the teasing tone, she looked so sad for a moment that the urge to put his arms around her almost overwhelmed him.

They were standing close together and he could feel the warmth emanating from her or maybe it was coming from him, because he certainly felt heated.

Impulsively he leant down and brushed her cheek with his lips. 'Thanks, Montana. I really appreciate your help.' Added very softly, 'Best fun I've had all year.'

When he kissed her forehead she tilted her face toward his. Her eyes seemed to be all he could see until he noticed her mouth. It looked so soft and curved and delightful...

He lowered his head and of course their lips met.

Just a fleeting, impersonal kiss. Or was it?

No, not impersonal. This was the first, brief, gentle touch of magic and the first breath of a new life, the first woman in his space since Jess, and while it was different from all that had gone before, it felt mystically right and wonderful.

Too wonderful. On his side anyway.

He stepped back and neither of them said anything. There was no need to talk or to take it further at this moment. But he'd certainly have to think about this later.

His mobile beeped softly and he moved away to listen and yet his eyes stayed on hers until he terminated the call. He threw the phone on the bed to get dressed. All the laughter was gone from her eyes.

'Do you want to come with me while I visit Emma's mother? She's had another fall. Emma said not urgent but I'll go now.'

'Sure. If you don't think I'll be in the way.'

He'd thrown on clothes over his jocks and pulled on his shirt. In seconds he stood at the door with his car keys in his hand.

'I can introduce you and say we were coming to meet them anyway.'

She said, 'Can we go by the kitchen and ask Louisa if she can listen for Dawn?'

Lucky one of them was thinking. Andy frowned at himself. 'Of course.'

# Montana

## CHAPTER THIRTEEN

Emma's parents lived opposite the lake in a rambling old farmhouse with wide verandas. The garden in the front yard exploded with roses and they passed under a bloom-laden arch spanning the path and bush after bush of colour amongst lush greenery and rocks.

'How beautiful. I love roses.' She turned back to Andy.

'I must show you Clare's Blue Moon. Palest lavender blue rose. Clare has them round the back.'

It seemed a strange thing to say, she thought. 'Why that one?'

'I saw a web page on rose meanings once,' he said cryptically, then changed the subject. 'Clare is an avid gardener, though she says even that isn't giving her pleasure at the moment.'

He frowned and Montana could see his thoughts had shifted to his patient. Emma opened the door at his knock and Montana noted how the young girl's stomach showed roundness more noticeably now.

Emma blinked when she saw Montana.

Andy loomed behind her. 'Hi, Emma. Montana and I were

together when you called. I hope you don't mind that I brought her.'

Emma shook her head. 'Of course not. Come in, both of you. Mum's in the lounge. She's still cross I called you.'

Andy patted her shoulder. 'You did the right thing. What happened?'

Emma brushed her hair out of her eyes. 'She was tying trellis in the back yard and she got tangled up in the ladder when she was coming down. She's getting worse. Her balance is off and she's so clumsy. Now I think she's got a twitch.'

Montana could see that Emma instinctively knew there was something seriously not right with her mother and Andy frowned at Emma's description as if something had triggered a thought.

He led the way to the lounge, where Clare was busy dusting the mantelpiece. As they came into the room a photo frame went flying off the mantelpiece and cracked in two on the floor.

Clare said, 'Blast!'

Emma looked at Andy and Montana as if to say, *See!*

Andy paused and studied Clare for a moment, and Montana saw the instant when the diagnosis suggested itself to him. He stiffened and then his shoulders slumped slightly before he pulled himself together.

He turned and met Montana's eyes and the shock she saw there made her draw a quick breath.

'What's wrong?' Emma was no slouch and she knew something significant had happened. She crossed to Andy and tugged at his sleeve. 'What is it? What's wrong with her?'

Clare turned, finally registering their presence, and Montana could see the tears in her eyes. 'Oh. Hello. Excuse me.' She picked up the broken frame. 'I hate this. I was never an uncoordinated person.'

She saw Montana and tried to smile. Andy repeated what he'd said to Emma about them being together. 'And I wanted to introduce you to Montana as she's helping Emma with her antenatal information.'

'Yes. I think Emma said something about that.' Clare made a visible effort to remember and held out her hand. Her fingers twitched a little as she put her hand in Montana's and smiled perfunctorily. 'It's nice to meet you.'

'You too,' Montana said.

Clare dropped Montana's hand as if she'd forgotten she held it and reached up to brush the tears from her face before she turned to Andy. 'Andy? What's happening to me?'

Andy patted Emma's hand and moved across to her mother. He put his arm around Clare and drew her back to the lounge. 'Please, sit down, Clare.' He quickly checked her over from her fall and then pulled a little torch from his pocket to check her pupils. 'Are you sore anywhere from your fall?'

'No, I'm fine.' She frowned at her daughter and then turned back to him. 'Emma shouldn't have bothered you.'

'I'm glad she did. She did the right thing.' He sighed as he watched her perch anxiously on the edge of the lounge and then he crouched down beside her.

'Is it stress? Causing this?' Clare looked at Andy as if she needed him to answer yes.

'I'm not sure, Clare. It could be a number of things, but we need to find the cause. We need a full physical examination and more blood tests. Maybe a trip to Brisbane.'

'Brisbane?' Vaguely.

He waited for a bigger response but Clare didn't react more so he pushed on. 'At first I thought your symptoms might have been from the car accident, but they aren't following the pattern I expected. Your fingers seem a little shakier today and there are some diseases that cause symptoms like yours. This particular one I'm thinking of can do that but it doesn't make sense yet.'

Clare looked up at him and compressed her lips as if to stop them trembling. 'I will get better though, won't I?'

'I'd need to do a blood test to know these things. Are your parents alive, Clare?'

Clare shook her head. 'They died in a car accident in their early thirties.'

'And their parents?'

'I'm not sure how they died.'

'Okay. We'll run some tests. Are you finding tasks more difficult? Do things you could normally do seem trickier now?'

Clare raised her eyes to his and nodded. 'Even getting dressed in the morning seems to take forever with these clumsy fingers.'

Andy rubbed the back of his neck. 'I'll chat to someone in Brisbane and we'll get some blood sent away for genetic testing. In the meantime, it might be better if you didn't drive the car.'

'Genetic testing?'

Clare heard that bit and the alarm in her eyes caused Andy to reach down and grip her hands in both of his in support. Montana could see that Andy shared his patient's distress.

Clare went on slowly, as if she dreaded to say the words, 'So if I had a genetic disease then my kids could have it?' She looked at Emma. 'And Emma's baby, too?'

Emma gasped and her hand slid protectively over her stomach. Montana slipped her arm around the young woman and squeezed her shoulders, suddenly glad she had come.

Andy clasped Clare's hands tightly once more before

sitting back to look into her face. 'I'm nowhere near sure that's what it is but we will find out. Let's not panic and get ahead of ourselves.' He spoke quietly but firmly. 'We'll do more tests. When the results come back we'll sort through the information. It could be something totally different. You will both have lots of questions and I'll make sure I can answer all of them.'

He looked at Emma and then back to Clare. 'Rest. And remember the more relaxed you are, the less the symptoms will be noticeable. Stress makes most medical conditions worse. I'll come back later and take some blood and I'll have a chat to my friend in Brisbane as well before I return.'

'I think I'll lie down,' Clare said, and she shook her head at Emma when she moved to help her. 'I'll be right by myself. Show Andy and his friend out, please, Emma.'

They said their goodbyes and as they drove away Montana examined Andy's profile. She ached for his silent distress. 'You think it could be chronic disease?'

'I had a sudden horrible fear it could be the onset of Huntington's disease. But that's way too scary to say out loud without proof.'

Montana's stomach dropped. She could still see the alarm in Emma's eyes as she'd watched them go. 'There's always a family history of Huntington's, isn't there?'

'True. Usually people have an idea they're at risk.' He flicked a glance at Montana. 'We have to remember that even if her mother proves positive for this inherited disease, there is the fifty per cent chance of it not being passed down to Emma or her baby.'

'Big leap without proof.'

Andy rubbed his face as if he found it difficult to show Montana even a little of what was churning him up inside. 'With no surviving older family, we can't deduce anything until we do testing. But I'm not liking the clinical picture. I've had this scenario before in Sydney so maybe the past is skewing my thoughts. I hope so.'

He shook his head as if disgusted with himself for taking so long to think of that answer. 'It would all make sense. The progression has been slow but the symptoms are there when you look, and it all slots into place.'

She could tell how upset he was by the risk of this coming true. 'What symptoms?' Montana wanted to do something to help Andy. 'It's all very vague.'

'She's had short-term memory loss, fidgeting, depression and apathy, which is so unlike Clare. Now that she has the involuntary movements in her fingers and toes, everything ties in.'

Montana puckered her forehead and then shook her head. 'I think you're being too hard on yourself. It's still pretty tenuous. I'd never have thought of Huntington's. It's not your everyday disease. And how could she not know about a family disease like that?' The link wasn't there, that Montana could see. 'Without the family history, Huntington's doesn't even come up.'

Andy rubbed the back of his neck again as if it ached. 'I think you'll find there will be an aunt or uncle or grandparent somewhere in the past who didn't die young. Obviously one of her parents had the gene but died in the car accident before they were diagnosed.'

'So it can't skip a generation?' Montana asked, and she shivered at Clare's prognosis.

'You're thinking of Emma and her baby again? And Emma's brothers.'

She nodded. 'It's a terrible thing to have hanging over your head.'

Andy watched the road intently and she had no doubt his

brain was racing. 'This disease usually doesn't manifest until the person is in their thirties or forties. It can even be as late as a person's seventies and in that case the disease is often mild.'

Best-case scenario, Montana prayed. 'So they could get it late and mild if they were lucky?'

Andy slapped the steering-wheel at the unfairness and Montana thought again how much she loved his empathy for his patients. 'Lucky? Yeah,' he said dryly.

They both fell silent as he drove another long country block before adding, 'I guess we have to think about some unfortunate people who have juvenile onset, but thankfully that's rare.'

Montana was thinking how hard this must be for Andy as a friend of the family. She didn't know how to comfort him or if he would accept such comfort. Best to keep it practical, she decided. The professional way. 'Can you treat Clare if this is what her problem is?'

He glanced across at her briefly and his face reflected his sombre thoughts. 'I will do everything I can for her and her family. We'll make sure they have the support they need but if Clare has inherited the gene then it's activated, and her central nervous system is breaking down. Her symptoms are only going to get worse and eventually she'll require full-time professional care.'

Montana stared at the road in front as the shock coursed through her. 'That's horrific.'

'The disease has a fairly slow progress and Clare could live another twenty years, a few of those fairly normally.'

'How few?'

He took one hand off the steering-wheel to rub his neck again and Montana wanted to slide her hand across his shoulders and gently soothe him herself.

'Clare will have enough warning,' he replied quietly, 'so she can modify her lifestyle and stay at home for as long as possible, but each year will be harder. We can all only pray someone finds a cure before then.'

The mood in the car was low and Montana thought again of Emma and her baby. 'Is there much hope for a cure?'

Andy turned and met her eyes briefly. 'There's always hope.'

And that there was Andy. Three words of a kind man who believed in life. 'So would you test Emma and her brothers?' She hoped he'd be spared the emotions of actual testing and diagnosis.

'We'd better make sure that's what it is first, but I'd suggest it, though the choice is up to them. It's not something they should rush into.' He exhaled a long breath, the sound heavy with feeling. 'Actually, I'd refer them to Brisbane for proper genetic counselling before the predictive test. I'd hate to let them down by wrong information or not enough correct information.'

Montana thought about it. 'I imagine some people would choose not to be tested until later in life so they can enjoy their life without confirmation of what's ahead. And some would decide not to tell their kids. Their decision.'

He nodded. 'The "let's worry about it if it happens," option, which has some positives going for it. Like Clare's parents. Other people feel they need to plan if they test positive. Either way it would have to colour your life. I'm darn sure of that!'

They pulled up at the house and Montana put her hand on his arm, left it there until he turned towards her. She weighed her words as if she had just realised a sudden truth. 'It puts living life to the full into perspective, doesn't it?'

There was a pause and Andy nodded. 'For me it does.'

They both heard his heartfelt response and she held her breath as he leaned towards her.

'Montana? Dawn's looking to be fed.' Louisa's voice broke the moment.

~

Later that evening, Montana heard Andy open the door out onto the veranda where she leaned against the rail.

Dark clouds obscured the moon and lightning flashed every few minutes and reflected off the lake's surface. A cool breeze rifled the hair back from her face as he came to stand beside her.

'Melancholy too?' he asked.

'That's an accurate description of how I'm feeling.' She turned to study his face. 'I can't stop thinking about Emma and what she has to go through with her mother, let alone the possibilities to herself.'

'Me too. If I thought railing at the universe would help I'd do it. I hate it. But we just have to wait for results.'

He slipped his arm around her shoulders and she could feel the comfort of his caring seep into her like a warm blanket of peace. She just hoped some comfort was going his way too because a lot of what she was feeling was because Andy was hurting so badly.

'We can only deal with the choice we're given. The amazing strength I see in patients and their families during hard times is why I love doing what I do.' He squeezed her shoulder and dropped his voice and she could hear his sincerity. 'It makes me humble.'

She rubbed the strong fingers that lay across her collarbone. To hear him talk about being humble made her want to throw her arms around him and pull his head down on her chest. His personal pain, the Andy as a man pain as opposed to the Dr Buchanan pain, for Clare and Emma and all their family made her heart ache.

He would have known them since he'd come here. Had only recently helped Emma's family come to terms with Emma's pregnancy. Now a terrible prognosis, debilitating and deadly was affecting them.

But he was right. They had to wait, and pray, and they would deal with the crappiest hands if they had to, and the world suddenly seemed a little less incomprehensible.

'Thank you,' she said quietly. 'You put that beautifully, Andy. I do understand. I've had patients who have awed me with their tenacity during a really hard labour and you feel so proud to have had a small part in their journey.'

He squeezed her shoulders one more time and then dropped his arm to lean on the rail beside her and gaze out over the lake. 'Who knows? You and I might have swapped a few more years with our loved ones for the risk of deterioration later in life — or maybe not. No one can tell how we'd react.'

She tried to recall the way Duncan had looked when one of his patients had had to endure hardship, but she couldn't. It hadn't been a big part of his make-up, but that was no excuse for not being able to remember. All she could see was Andy, hurting for Emma's family. All she could feel was this overpowering need to comfort him.

She tried harder to picture her late husband but nothing came. The thought horrified her and the expression of it came out in a hoarse whisper. 'I'm having trouble remembering Duncan's face.'

Andy looked down at her and brushed her cheek with his finger. 'Don't beat yourself up. It's tough when that starts to happen. I watched a movie once when someone said it helps if you remember a special moment in time rather than just their face. That works for me when I want to remember my wife.'

'Thank you. I'll try that.' It was odd how she could talk about Duncan with Andy but strangely didn't feel as comfortable for him to talk about his wife.

In fact she'd prefer that he didn't and she did not know why.

A week later Clare's results came back positive for Huntington's disease. Her family and in fact the whole town reeled with shock.

Emma had gone into caring mode for her mother and was even reluctant to leave long enough to talk to Montana about her pregnancy. It was as if she didn't want to think about the future too much and by being busy she could ignore what was hanging over her mother's and her own baby's head.

Montana understood that and suggested when Emma was ready she could go to Clare's house and do the antenatal mornings. Clare had asked if she could bring Dawn as well so she could watch her play.

From Montana's perspective, this was the perfect solution although she feared it would be bittersweet for Clare.

Would she ever get to see her grandchild? To hold her? To watch her play?

The thought was too awful to contemplate

# Montana

## CHAPTER FOURTEEN

In April, when the weather began to cool in the evenings, Montana started work as the new deputy nurse manager at the hospital.

Her tenure consisted of two four-hour administrative days per week to organise the new caseload midwifery unit and one eight-hour clinical day as the registered nurse on duty for the hospital. For the moment, Louisa had asked if she could babysit Dawn, but Montana was looking into a creche system they could run to help all staff with children. Dawn would become more of a handful soon enough and she didn't want Louisa to feel trapped into childminding. It would be a draw card for new recruits as well.

On her first morning as a nurse she worked with Chrissie, who welcomed her with no small degree of excitement and lots of practical help.

Chrissie was superwoman as far as Montana was concerned.

'You work full time and your husband is away three or four nights a week?' She shook her head at the red-headed pocket rocket. 'Chrissie. How do you manage?'

Chrissie laughed. 'My mum gets my son off to school and my husband helps on weekends so that's a bonus.'

Montana thought she made it sound a lot easier than it was. 'What's he do?'

'He's a truck whisperer.'

'A what? I've never heard that.'

Chrissie smiled reminiscently. 'That's what he told me when we met. He's really a diesel mechanic but he told me that trucks have emotional problems, just like horses.'

'Seriously?'

'He's Irish and has kissed the Blarney stone, so yeah, seriously. But I love him. When other mechanics can't find the fault, he's the one who goes in and sorts it out. He travels all over. His reputation is spreading faster than he can keep up.'

Montana smiled at the mental picture of an Irishman talking to a tractor about its emotional problems. 'He sounds super-busy. That must make to hard to balance your workloads and family time. Especially when he's away.'

Chrissie shrugged. 'We're saving up for a farm and then he'll be able to stay home and work from there. Be the home dad. Maybe we'll even have more kids.'

Andy's unmistakable step in the corridor heralded his arrival. 'What's this about you having more kids, Chrissie?'

'Not yet, I'm not and you'll be the last to know.' Chrissie joked, looking him up and down. 'You back again, Andy?'

Surprisingly, Andy had dropped in three times before eight in the morning for reasons Montana assumed she'd work out later.

She saw the twinkle in Chrissie's eye as she watched each of Andy's new explanations float past.

'How are you going, Montana?' Andy asked as he skimmed an outpatient chart.

'It's all pretty simple really,' Montana said as she checked expiry dates on medications and restocked dressing packs. Between the occasional outpatient who appeared for dressings or injections, Chrissie had spent their first hours together turning out drawers and cupboards so Montana knew where to find supplies when needed.

'Apart from the occasional disaster,' Chrissie warned, hands on hips. 'We do the best we can with what we have; the rest is more like a clinic than an emergency department. Speaking of clinics, how come yours is finished over at the house, Andy?'

'It's not. I just came over for some more X-ray forms. I'll see you later,' he said, and sauntered off again.

Chrissie put another empty box in the bin. 'The man's mad, but I have to thank him because having you here is so great. Even if you work part-time I'll have more flexibility with my shifts, which will thrill my family.' She opened another box. 'Imagine if more new staff came! Just having one more midwife on the books helps so much. Poor Rhonda has been out of it for too long and she's over having to be responsible for new babies if one drops in.'

Montana couldn't imagine ever being over midwifery. 'Has Andy told you about the new birthing centre plans?'

Chrissie nodded enthusiastically. 'He mentioned a little and it sounds great. Especially when I think about having another baby myself. Imagine if I didn't have to go away and wait for labour. Imagine if I could have the same person care for me the whole way through.'

'That's how caseload works and we want to drum up business. I think you should spread the word,' Montana teased. 'Andy's sister is a midwife and one of my best friends. I'm nagging her to pay a visit so I can talk to her about relocating to the lake.'

Chrissie stopped what she was doing and leant against the

bench to study Montana's face. 'Have you known Andy for a long time?' she asked casually.

Montana kept stocking boxes but she heard the curiosity in the words. 'No. I've worked with Misty for the last four years and she's one of my best friends, so I knew about her brother. Just hadn't met. 'I met Andy when he was in Coffs on a working holiday, at our base hospital there. This was shortly after my baby was born so I was on a working holiday too,' she said wryly. 'I needed a change and the timing was perfect. He suggested I come here to recuperate when I said I needed to get away.'

'Interesting.' Chrissie sounded thoughtful. 'He never loses an opportunity for new staff. I guess the Lake is a peaceful place.'

As she finished her sentence the wail of an approaching siren drifted in the window and they looked at each other and smiled in synchronicity.

'Spoke too soon,' Montana said.

'That'll bring Andy back again and it's not even nine o'clock,' Chrissie added with a smile.

Montana shut the cupboard she'd been arranging and moved towards the emergency bay. 'You see a lot of him over here, don't you?'

'Some days more than others,' Chrissie said cryptically, and came to stand beside her as they waited.

The siren turned out to be a police car carrying Chrissie's eight-year-old son, Dylan, who had fallen off his bike on the way to school. His left arm was swollen at the wrist and he began to cry in earnest when he saw his mother. The policeman and his wife, Bob and June, had scooped him from the road and June had him on her lap while her husband drove.

June was almost as upset as Dylan.

They immobilised the arm, lifted him off June's lap and carried him into the observation room. The boy's tear-streaked face made Montana want to hug him to her and she wondered at Chrissie's ability to console Dylan and still arrange for the retired technician to come in and X-ray her son's arm. She wasn't sure she'd have been so sane if Dawn had been the one hurt.

Montana had plied Bob and June with tea for their nerves and cemented a new relationship with two more lovely people of the Lake.

An hour later the results were through and Andy was happy to manage Dylan conservatively. 'Even though his radius and ulna are cracked, the base hospital has confirmed it won't need surgery,' Andy said. 'We'll give him a sedative and the cast will give enough support for it to heal. I'll write a referral for the orthopaedic surgeon for a check next week, and when he wakes up you can take him home and look after him.'

Chrissie sighed. 'Poor baby. He'll go berserk with boredom if he can't be a daredevil.' She looked at Montana. 'Sorry I have to leave you on day one. So much for helping you settle in.'

'I'll be fine,' Montana reassured her. 'I've learnt the essentials this morning. I can call Andy or talk to you on the phone. And Bill will be here after lunch when he starts his shift. I can save any questions I have for him.'

Now Montana was in charge of the cottage hospital but there were no more moments of unusual interest for the rest of the day. Just two old dears in the medical end who wanted to know what had happened with the siren. She brought them up to speed and made another two friends at the lake.

Andy brought Dawn over to her mother at lunchtime as Louisa was immersed in the kitchen, cooking for Ned's surprise party the following week. They spent an agreeable half-hour discussing who would come to the party.

Montana was back home by four and felt pleasantly satisfied with her first day. The small town feel and connections in the tiny hospital were so different to those in Coffs Harbour, which was more a busy referral centre.

When she walked into the kitchen, Andy jiggled Dawn on his lap and Montana shook her head in disbelief. Home already? 'I can't believe how many times I've seen you today.'

Andy looked at Dawn, not at her. 'I know. Crazy, isn't it?' he said into her daughter's hair.

He looked almost embarrassed but she couldn't pin down why. But, oh the sight of him playing with Dawn brought an odd bubble of happiness to her chest. 'One of us is silly. What do you think, Dawn? Is it mummy or Uncle Andy?'

She smiled at Andy, teasing, then, with sudden clarity, Montana realised she was flirting with the man holding her baby. They had said life was there for living but her baby was so young and her husband gone for just under a year.

Further words dried on her tongue. Was she ready for flirting? She didn't even know that. Life was unfair and too confusing and she needed to get away from him before she really embarrassed herself and burst into tears.

'I'll take Dawn. Excuse me,' she said, and left the room rapidly with her daughter.

It was the night of Ned's seventieth birthday.

After several early-morning hours of self-talk about the fickleness and tragedy of life Montana cited her and Andy's loss and Clare's shock diagnosis she admonished herself for being a drama queen and for allowing herself to wallow in guilt. As the hour drew near for the big event, she vowed to enjoy the evening and the attention of Andy, if it came her way, without regret.

And she couldn't wait to see him in the new kilt and jacket.

Ned was a truly delightful man and she wished him a great party. She would not bring any of her heartache along to ruin his evening, though she would probably be late if she didn't soon decide on an outfit. She'd spent far too much time fantasising about how Andy would look in his kilt and none about how to dress herself.

In the end, she chose a black skirt and white lacy top with a frilled neckline. If it looked a little like it could go with a tartan cape, so what? It didn't mean anything, right?

Ned was due back from his regular chess game at seven and the guests were arriving from six-thirty to six forty-five so as to be hidden by seven. Montana glanced at her watch. Six. Half an hour until the guests started to arrive. She wanted to slip into the kitchen to see if she could help with any last-minute chores.

She'd just settled Dawn down for a sleep when Andy knocked softly on her door. 'You there, Montana?' His voice was low but she heard the words clearly. Funny, that.

Her heart tripped a little as she took a deep breath and opened her door.

Oh my. She almost forgot to breathe out. He looked incredibly handsome in his new clothes. To say her measuring had been successful was a huge understatement.

'Well? Is that a good open-mouthed stare or a bad one? Say something.' His face twitched and he wasn't smiling. She couldn't believe he was unsure. He didn't need to be nervous.

'Oh, my goodness,' was all she could say, and even that

came out muffled because one hand had flown up to cover her open mouth.

Andy stared back anxiously. 'Do I look silly?'

'Silly isn't a word that leaps to mind.' Her heart swooped and dived in her chest like the aerobatic plane Andy wanted her to climb into. She met his eyes and dragged her hand away and smiled. 'No. You look amazing. Fabulous. A mighty fine Scot.'

His shoulders dropped with relief. 'Och, aye, then.' He grinned and twirled his yellow and red kilt. 'I still can't decide whether to wear jocks or not.'

She blinked and her face flushed at the thought. 'You're kidding me, right?'

His grin widened. 'Yeah, but I had you worried.'

Kill that thought. But, of course, she couldn't. She felt like a kid waking up on her birthday, full of excitement at opening a special gift.

But that was silly.

It was Ned's birthday.

'That's a relief. I was worried for the innocent children if you got carried away with the Highland Reel and fell over later.'

'You are a hard woman, Montana Browne.'

He may have said 'hard' but he'd said it softly and the inflection didn't correlate with the word. His gaze lingered on her face and goose bumps raised all over her body. She needed space, she needed breath, and she forced herself to move out of the danger zone.

'You look cute in a skirt,' she said to lighten the tone, 'but I have to go and see if I can do something for poor Louisa in the kitchen. She's working herself up into a state, I'm sure.'

'A kilt, woman, not a skirt. Please.'

She smiled back, pleased that he'd picked up her tone. Light and easy. Just friends, enjoying the banter.

Andy glanced at his watch. 'What about you and I take over the kitchen from Louisa so she can go and change and put on her make-up before Ned arrives? Chrissie has come over to meet people at the door and hide them in the library until seven.'

'Good idea. Lead on, MacDuff!'


In the kitchen, Louisa laughed so hard at the kilt that in the end Montana felt sorry for Andy.

'Watch you don't lay an egg there, Louisa.' Andy pretended to be miffed. 'Off you go and pretty yourself up. We'll look after things here and meet you in the library at five to seven.'

Louisa scurried out, dragging off her apron as she went, but she still giggled.

Montana glanced at Andy's crestfallen face as she stirred through a bowl of rice salad. 'Poor Andy. She laughed at you.'

Andy scooped coleslaw into a large crystal dish. 'I prefer to think she laughed with me, if you don't mind.'

Manfully she swallowed a snort. Carefully placed a sprig of parsley in the middle of her bowl and then Andy's for garnish. Said to the dish instead of the gorgeous man. 'I think you look wonderful.'

'That's all that matters, then.'

He said it lightly but when Montana looked at him again he stood very still, watching her. She turned away to the sink to hide her flushed cheeks. There was more to that statement than she'd first realised. And it gave her butterflies.

'By the way...' He was right behind her when she turned

back. He had a sprig of parsley in his hand and he held it over their heads. 'It's not mistletoe but it will do.'

'What—?'

She didn't finish because he'd pulled her gently into his arms and kissed her. Only a gentle kiss but this time there was a hint of promise that he had further plans. She didn't know what she thought of that and there wasn't time to think about it now.

'I needed that for my bruised ego,' was all he said when he released her.

She frowned. 'You're getting a little too easy with your kisses. Glad I could be of service, but a little warning wouldn't go astray.' *Don't read too much into it*, she told herself. 'We should move to the library because I think I just heard Joe's car arrive to drop off Ned.'

Andy looked horrified. 'You can hear outside noises while I'm kissing you?' He shook his head as he popped the salads into the fridge. 'That's not a good recommendation of my technique.'

'We will talk about your technique later.' Which is pretty damn good, she added silently. 'Let's go or we'll miss the surprise.'

They slipped into the darkened library, past Chrissie who raised her eyebrows at Andy's kilt, and then everyone grew silent as they heard the front door open.

'Of course you can come in, Joe.' Ned sounded jovial and Montana suspected he might even have had a whisky to help with his chess game. He went on as another voice could be heard on the veranda. 'Louisa can always set another place at the table. Now, where is everybody?'

'In here, Ned,' Andy called out, and they waited in the darkness for the door to open.

A shaft of light preceded Ned's face as he peered around

the door and into the room. 'Has the bulb blown?' he asked and flicked the switch.

'Surprise!' Twenty smiling faces appeared with the light and Ned took a step back and clutched his chest.

'A dinna ken what you're doin' here.' He lapsed into broad Scots and Andy patted his back.

'It's all right, old timer. It's a surprise party for your seventieth. Don't have a heart attack on us.'

'Well, what do you expect? A bunch of noddies like you in the dark would scare anyone.' He looked Andy up and down. 'Andy, me boy. You've found yourself a kilt. You look bonny.'

'In honour of you.' Andy rotated to show it off.

'I appreciate that. I really do. You should have had one sooner.' Ned looked around. 'Now, where's that lass of yours?'

'Would that be me?' Montana smiled and kissed Ned's cheek. 'Many happy returns, Ned.'

'Thank you, sweetheart.'

'Don't thank me. Louisa has been slaving in secret for weeks.'

He turned to Louisa with a soft smile. 'Now you are my true sweetheart.' Ned put his hand out to the older woman and pulled her forward. 'Dear Louisa. Thank you.'

He planted a gentle kiss on his housekeeper's startled lips and winked at Andy.

Music started in the background, a Scottish reel that Ned loved, and he towed Louisa forward. 'I'm afraid I'm a bit slow in one hip but now that I'm a decent age I'll no let grass grow under my feet. Shall we dance, lass?'

Ned twirled a laughing Louisa into the middle of the floor and the party began. Montana stepped back and watched with a smile on her face until Andy came up behind her and pulled her back against his body.

'We need to check the kitchen,' he said into her ear and

Montana didn't know which sensation to register first. The feel of his hard body against her back or the fluttery jangle of nerves he'd sent to her stomach with his whispery breath.

She shouldn't be registering either. Should she?

She pulled away and stood straight again. 'Lead the way. We can get the food out onto the table in the hall and open all the doors.'

Andy frowned and followed. 'Then we can talk about my technique.'

Chrissie came up behind them. 'What technique would that be, Andy?' There was a bubble of laughter in her voice and Montana stifled a giggle. Andy was having a poor evening being the butt of everyone's jokes.

Always quick with an answer, Andy said, 'A new surgical tie, Chrissie. Where are you going?'

Chrissie looked surprised. 'I'm coming to help Montana in the kitchen, of course.'

Andy nodded as if he'd suspected she might be. 'Then I'm off to drink to Ned's health.'

# Andy

## CHAPTER FIFTEEN

Andy slipped out to the veranda because suddenly he didn't feel like partying.

There'd been a few occasions when he'd thought that Montana felt the same way he did or at least had begun to be attracted to him. Then she would step back or deliberately misinterpret his intent and he'd be back at square one.

He'd become way too attracted to the maddening woman to get himself out of the nowhere land he seemed stuck in.

In the three years since his wife had died he hadn't looked at another woman until Montana burst into his life. Losing Jess had rocked his world. The whole time she'd been sick he'd assumed the cancer would be beaten, that their lives would eventually come back on track and his darling Jess would return to health.

That hadn't happened, and when she'd gone downhill so fast at the end he'd felt like he'd been trying to hold a hurtling train from dashing over a cliff.

But despite all his years devoted to medicine, his professional contacts and the centre of excellence he'd taken her to, Jess had died.

Everything and everyone had failed her. He'd failed her.

And he'd thought he would never feel whole again.

Now Montana had healed him and he was ready to think about happiness and life again.

She and her gorgeous daughter had broken through the shell around his heart with her courage and her serenity. The last thing he wanted was to damage that serenity by making a nuisance of himself. He needed to proceed slowly or he would scare her off, but it was hard when he knew how cruel life could be and he wanted to live.

Live life with Montana and Dawn.

Love with Montana and Dawn.

When that all-too-brief kiss had hinted at the passion brewing between them he'd known he was right.

He'd never thought he would feel that kind of connection with anyone again. But with Montana, he had.

When he went back to the party half an hour later, Montana was dancing with Chrissie's husband and Andy leant against the wall and watched.

What was it about this woman that affected him so deeply?

Her dark hair was confined in an ornate clasp and the slender column of her throat rose from her shoulders like the stem of flower. The hollow beneath her ear and her jaw made him want to draw her in and rest his fingers on that flushed delicate skin. Just to feel it. Inhale her scent there.

He pushed himself off the wall and was considering returning outside when she looked up, smiled and crooked her finger at him.

His ridiculous heart jumped. 'Your wish is my command,' he murmured to himself, and moved towards her.

Chrissie's husband stepped back with a grin and suddenly Andy had what he wanted — Montana in his arms, and the chance to hold her close without needing an excuse. She relaxed into his embrace as if she'd been waiting for him, and he wondered if that was true or wishful thinking on his part.

Either way, her body fit perfectly with his, and he held her lightly, barely needing to guide her as their steps matched the dance movements.

'Where did you go?' she asked above the music. 'We looked for you after we finished in the kitchen.'

'Stargazing. But the view is just as magical in here. Did I mention how beautiful you look tonight?'

You feel beautiful, he added silently, as he leant down to draw in her subtle perfume. It was as intoxicating as he'd remembered. Somehow, he resisted the urge to brush that sensitive skin under her ear with his lips.

'I think you look magnificent in your kilt, Dr Buchanan.'

'Magnificent, eh? That sounds promising.'

'Let's just dance.' She leant her cheek against his chest and he gathered her closer and closed his eyes. She was right they needed to just dance.

After the party, when all the revellers had departed and the mess had been cleaned up, Montana disappeared before he could say goodnight. Okay. She needed time.

He went for a fast walk along the lake to clear — or was that cool — his mind?

It didn't work.

Back in his room he dropped the kilt, jacket and shirt, and

wrapping his towel around his waist strode down the hallway to the bathroom.

Everyone else was in bed and probably sleeping the sleep of the innocent. He was anything but that.

Tonight he wanted Montana and he pulled back the screen and stepped into the shower, blasting his skin with a dousing of cold water. He shuddered as the onslaught beat against his chest and ran icily over his belly, but he knew it was the only way there was a chance he'd be able to sleep.

He twisted the tap to hot and then cold again and then hot and cold again until he stood at last with the cold water pelting him into submission.

He sighed, reached and turned the tap off, then slung the towel around his waist and took himself to bed.

## *Montana*

### CHAPTER SIXTEEN

Montana tried being busy to avoid thinking. It wasn't working.

She'd taken to spending long hours in the evenings, when Dawn was asleep, on her computer to assemble procedures and protocols for the setup of the stand-alone caseload midwifery unit. A lot of the paperwork she adapted from what she'd prepared before, which had been sent across by Misty from Coffs Harbour. Apart from the state differences, the main area of organisation was in the transportation of women should medical need arise.

Andy was a general practitioner with his obstetric diploma so he could give medical back-up prior to transfer, but they needed seamless access to an obstetric service for sick mums and babies. The base would hopefully supply that but Montana needed to set up networking so seamless emergency transfer left everyone on the same page.

The reams of paperwork kept her out of Andy's way. Exhaustion helped too. Combined, they didn't leave enough time to think about her disloyalty to Duncan.

Her conscience screamed that her growing feelings for

Andy were indecently early. She shouldn't even be thinking of another man as she approached the first anniversary of her husband's death.

~

That day, the first of May, was fittingly cool and grey in Lyrebird Lake.

It fell on a Friday and she'd agreed to do a shift for Chrissie who wanted to go away for the weekend with her family. Working seemed like a good way to get through part of the long gloomy day. She didn't mention the significance of the day to anyone at the Lake, possibly because she didn't want to talk about her feelings, though she had spoken to Misty and Mia that morning when they'd rung to see how she was.

When the shift was over, she borrowed Louisa's car and drove herself and Dawn up the winding road to the lookout where she gazed out over the town. A town that she realised she'd grown very fond of and could see being her home for a long time to come if things continued down the road she could see ahead.

She lifted a picnic blanket from the back of the car and made a place for her and Dawn on the mountainside. Her fingers curled in the grass under her. Dawn lay gazing at the tree they sat under, watching glimpses of sky from her blanket.

Montana blew out a gust of guilt and concentrated on memories of her husband. He had been a good man, a good husband and would have been a good father. She hoped somewhere he could look down and see his beautiful daughter. See her growing more like Montana every day with his firm mouth.

'I can't believe it's already a year since you left, Duncan,' she said to the sky, and shook her head.

She cuddled Dawn against her and sighed. It didn't feel as though anyone was listening, and she wanted to believe this was a good thing. That he was at rest, not haunting her. That he would want her to get on with her life, find new love, but she couldn't staunch the feeling of guilt.

The distant sound of another car as it climbed the hill penetrated her reverie and she turned to watch it park beside hers.

She'd known it was Andy even before she'd seen his vehicle.

He walked across to her and she wasn't sure if she was glad or sorry he had come. 'I'm sorry if I'm intruding but I've been worried about you all day. The anniversary of your loss.'

Misty must have rung him. That's the only way he could know and now that he did...

His compassion made her want to weep all over him and she really didn't want to do that. She tried to talk but her throat closed up. Shaking her head in distress, she looked away.

'Just tell me to go and I will,' he said softly.

'Stay,' she managed finally. 'Maybe you can help. I'm just so confused that I feel this way when a year ago I thought I would never be happy again.'

He looked at her swiftly and then away, as if afraid of the answer. 'Apart from the obvious sadness of today, are you happy?'

'I love it here,' she confessed. 'The town, the people. Dawn is thriving. Life shouldn't be this good only a year after Duncan's death.'

Andy rubbed his neck. 'What is the right time to start living, to feel happiness after a loss like that? It's hard.'

He'd turned to face her and she could see he felt strongly about this. She supposed he would, given he'd been through the same loss.

'Everyone is different. You knew to get away was the best thing for you and Dawn and I believe with all my being that you did the right thing.'

She tried to explain the confusing array of emotions at war inside her. 'I can't deal with this guilt that I'm too fickle. That it's indecent of me to be almost healed. To want a new life for Dawn and I. To look at happy families and want that for us. To look at you and feel so at ease. He's only been gone a year.'

She looked up into his face, and his eyes said that he did understand. Andy always understood. 'For some people a new life might not come along for ten years but for others it arrives within months. There are no rules to say you haven't suffered enough. You just have to be strong enough to grab it when it comes.'

He crouched down before continuing. 'Jess has been gone three years. For me, it's taken all of that time. Or maybe it's not measurable in time, maybe it's measurable in the person I needed to meet. Either way, the fact is that I've met you. And when you're ready to talk, so am I. But today isn't the day for that.'

She looked at him and saw the man he was. Saw his understanding and lack of impatience, and knew she could grace herself with some slack to not rush into anything.

Their eyes met and held and for the first time that day she felt some semblance of peace. 'Thank you,' was all she needed to say. Andy understood.

.  .  .

A week later Emma arrived at the doctors' house for another antenatal class. She'd rung, said her dad was home with her mum, and she wanted to have the class at Ned's.

'I'm glad you could come,' Montana said when Emma hugged her.

'I wanted to come.' She looked around the familiar room and then back at Montana. 'It is good to see you, too, and get out of the house.'

Montana followed her into the room. 'Sit. Unwind. How are your father and mother?'

They sat at the table where Montana had set up cold drinks and savoury biscuits, and Emma stopped pacing and sank into a chair. Her shoulder sagged and she closed her eyes for a moment.

When she opened her eyes she smiled. A little sadly but it was a real smile nonetheless. 'Dad's pretty amazing, really. He's already made the house safer and easier to maintain for Mum, which will help her cut back on accidents. He keeps telling her he loves her and he will love her forever, no matter what. That sounds a bit cheesy when I say it out loud, but it's not. It's pretty sweet.'

'Your dad is wonderful,' Montana said softly.

Emma's eyes welled with sudden tears. 'If I have the gene then no one will have the chance to love me like that. I won't let them.'

Oh, dear. This wasn't just about her parents. Something or someone had upset her badly. 'What has Tommy said?'

Emma threw her head up. 'He said his mother reckons we should terminate the pregnancy. Or adopt the baby out.'

Her hands cupped protectively over her baby like they had the day Andy had diagnosed her mother. 'How can people say things like that about *my* baby?'

Poor Emma. And Tommy.

'Nobody can force you to give up your baby, Emma. And you're thirty weeks. Termination is off the table. Some people say hurtful things when they're scared.' She squeezed the girl's hand. 'You'll have to pretend she didn't say it. One day, hopefully, you can forgive her.'

Emma's lip quivered and Montana ached to be able to comfort her. 'There's a big chance you don't have the gene, Emma. Even if you do, your baby has just as big a chance of not having it.'

Emma brushed her hand across her eyes, scrubbing the wetness away. 'I'm not even thinking about me and it's too far away to think about when my child is thirty. It's when my baby is threatened now. How could she even say that?' She threw out a hand. 'Tommy's not even talking to her anymore.'

Montana poured the cold lemonade, slices of lime bobbing in it with the ice, and handed Emma a glass. She wanted to let the emotion of the outburst subside before she continued. 'When your baby is born,' she said after Emma had taken a long drink, 'Tommy's mother will want to be involved too, and she should be. A grandchild is a wonderful joy in life. Tommy's mother is just not as strong as you at the moment and she will regret her comments when she meets your baby. But everything takes time.'

Emma blew out a breath and nodded and Montana went on. 'In less than ten weeks your gorgeous baby will be here and you will be an awesome mother.'

Emma dropped her voice. 'I don't know anything about looking after a baby. How will I know what to do?'

Montana smiled. 'Nobody does until they do it. When you come in to have your baby we'll help you practise caring for her before you go home. Then we'll visit you at home and help with anything you need help with. But you'll learn fast because you'll love your baby.' Montana lowered her voice.

'Don't underestimate that you still have your mother to help you learn to mother your baby as well.'

'I know. One of my friends' mothers was killed in an accident three years ago. She said I'm lucky I still have my mum.' She sniffed and visibly shook off her distress. 'I really don't want to waste Mum's good times worrying about the not so good ones to come. That's why I came here today.'

'That's very thoughtful and wise of you, Emma.'

She looked Montana in the eye. 'I am glad I came because I knew I could talk about things with you. Things I can't say to other people. Saying it out loud helps me clear my mind.'

Montana hugged her. 'Your baby is one lucky little girl... Or boy.' She stepped back, brushed her eyes, and sniffed. 'I'd better blow my nose and get on with it, then. It's time we discussed labour.'

# Andy

## CHAPTER SEVENTEEN

Andy sat reading the paper on the veranda, or trying to, but the conversation floated out to him and he couldn't help overhearing. Poor Emma. Poor Montana, because she was fond of Emma, too.

He felt like strangling Tommy's mother but instead he'd better go and see if he could talk some sense into her. He had an hour and a half until Louisa served the evening meal. If he did half as well as Montana had with Emma, it would be worth the effort.

As he drove he shook his head at the amazing conversation he'd overheard. It made him see Montana again and what she'd brought to the Lake and to him.

If only he could use that same rationale with her in regard to getting on with life. Her husband would never return and life was too precarious to waste opportunities such as they had, but he knew she felt it was too soon to move onto a new relationship.

Yet he could see how amazing life could be for the two of them and for Dawn and he wanted Montana to see that, too.

He needed advice, or someone else to talk to her. He'd

thought he'd done a damn fine job in being understanding about Montana's wishes and her needing to take more time. It had been a long time since he'd tried to talk to a woman with a view to commitment. Was he going about it all wrong?

Maybe he should ring his sister tonight, get some advice or see when she was coming to visit, even if he had to fly down and get her himself.

On Friday, when Montana had finished her first well-women's clinic at the hospital, Andy appeared in her office after the last patient had left. He allowed himself the luxury of admiring her as she organised her desk.

Her hair was tied back in a shiny clasp and several dark wisps tickled her cheek. He wanted to brush them back with his fingers and make her see how good the two of them would be together. Now that he'd come to realise how much Montana meant to him, he was desperate for her to see it too. But he didn't want to destroy the fragile relationship they had with his impatience.

'Montana, a question?' he said softly, not to startle her, and Montana looked up at his voice. The unguarded, welcoming smile on her face reassured him. They were progressing.

She straightened and brushed the hair away from her cheek. 'Hello, there, Dr Buchanan. Yes?'

He walked over and looked at the list of patients she'd seen that day. It was a long one. It seemed a fair proportion of the townswomen had avoided their yearly checks until Montana had arrived.

As he stood beside her he could just catch the faintest hint of the lavender soap she used. Going into the bathroom at home after Montana was always a struggle because that scent left a vivid picture in his mind. This woman, naked, lathering her body...

She stretched her neck to look up at him and he was oh so tempted to kiss those teasing lips.

'We're to be formal, then, nurse? And I was going to ask you something very informal.' Her perfect brows went up and he smiled and went on. 'It's your first clinic. Let's celebrate at the only restaurant in town tonight. Dinner. Just the two of us.'

'Like a date?' She was teasing him again. Good. Let's get it out there.

'Not *like* a date.' He paused and she tilted her head, looking confused. He could see she'd missed the point. 'A date. Dinner, dancing, table service. Say yes.'

Montana blinked. 'They have dancing?'

He smiled. 'They have a romantic opera collection on CD and a handkerchief-sized dance floor.'

She looked away and he couldn't catch her expression. 'Ask Louisa if she would mind Dawn, do you mean?'

She turned back to him and he watched different emotions cross her face as she considered the logistics. Why couldn't she just say yes and work out the details later?

Then she did. 'I'd like that, Andy. If Louisa isn't busy, it would be nice to get dressed up a little and have a meal out.'

'With me.' He clarified the situation because he needed her to get it.

'With you, yes.' She smiled at him as the idea grew. Just like the pleasure that expanded in his own chest. It felt good to hear her say yes. 'What time?'

'Say... six-thirty for seven?'

She nodded.

'We can have a leisurely meal, a few turns around the

floor.' Already he was planning. He wanted to relive that feeling of Montana in his arms. 'We'd still not be home too late for Dawn.'

Maybe walk along the lake afterwards and watch the submarine races, he thought, but didn't add that. This was such a good idea. A date shifted the platonic colleague thing into a whole new area. It sent the message he wanted to make.

Silently he thanked Misty for suggesting this as his next move.

Please universe it would go as well in practice as in planning. Because in the last few weeks he'd been going quietly insane.

# *Montana*

## CHAPTER EIGHTEEN

Montana was ready early because she'd learnt that babies tended to have last-minute moments of unusual interest and she didn't want to keep Andy waiting.

He found her in the kitchen with Dawn at six-fifteen, dressed and ready, and she blushed at the way his eyes lit up when he saw her.

She'd pampered herself in the bathroom and then spent extra time drying her hair so that it bounced freely around her neck — a big change, as she rarely left her hair down. Tonight, it had seemed like the thing to do. The straps on her apricot blouse left her shoulders bare and the floral skirt swirled when she twirled in her strappy sandals.

All those things, and the way Andy looked at her, made her feel especially feminine tonight and it was a giddy feeling she'd forgotten.

Dawn waved them goodbye, with a little help from Louisa, and they walked under the streetlights the three short blocks to the restaurant. The breeze from the lake seemed especially soft on this mild May night.

Andy caught her hand and held it and she left her fingers

there, warm and secure in his, and tried to ignore the flutter of tension caused by that connection.

Only holding hands, she told herself. That is not a commitment.

The Paragon, the only restaurant in Lyrebird Lake, was run by Angelo and Angelina, an eccentric Italian couple who supplemented the menu they loved to serve with a pizza take-away.

In the main restaurant, to Montana's surprise, the room was dim with dripping candles in basketed Chianti bottles and red-checked tablecloths. Romantic Italian opera played softly in the background and she smiled at the memory of Andy's forewarning. The only other couple in the room were being served their meal with a voluble flourish as Montana and Andy arrived, and the little Italian looked torn between the two tasks.

'We'll seat ourselves, Angelo. No hurry, please,' Andy said, ushering Montana to a secluded corner where a sheaf of long purple roses lay across the table. He smiled as he pulled her chair out, then tilted his head towards the Italian. 'Angelo likes to explain the meal when he serves it, and I didn't want to spoil his fun.'

Montana lifted the roses before she sat down. Andy being thoughtful again? Always. She inhaled the exquisite scent. 'Did you send these in for me?'

'From Clare's garden. I picked them up earlier. I swear she has every colour you could imagine.'

Her brows drew together as a memory teased her. 'I'm sure you mentioned a special meaning for purple roses before.'

'Later,' he said, and seated her with such care she might have been a celebrity or movie star. Andy could hold his own with anyone on the big screen so she had the right dinner partner.

She brushed her hand over the cutlery, as if the coldness of the silver would rid her head of silly thoughts. Or at least bring her back to earth.

The tantalising aroma of herbs and garlic made Montana's mouth water and she let Andy's reason for purple roses slip away for later. For the first time in months she realised how hungry she was. In fact, she hadn't really been interested in what she'd eaten since her loss. Maybe that was all a part of feeling so alive and vital tonight.

The Paragon was a classical Italian restaurant and she loved every detail. She could not wait to see the menu. 'Thank you for bringing me here.' She smiled at Andy as he settled on the opposite side of the table.

'My pleasure.' He bowed and gave her one of those gorgeous hundred-watt smiles that made her cheeks glow before he flicked his napkin onto his lap.

Montana settled back in her chair and sighed happily as she looked around. 'This is wonderful, Andy. The food looks and smells amazing, and we could be in any restaurant in Rome.'

They both looked across at the dapper Italian in his black shiny trousers, bow-tie and white apron. His hands gesticulated floridly as he explained intricate details to the other couple.

'He's a gem. Believe it or not, Angelo grew up around here. His parents immigrated many years ago and ran a huge property about fifty kilometres out of town.

'Angelo travelled to Italy to study under a master chef in Rome. There he met Angelina, who is also a chef. They had four sons in five years but came back when his parents needed help on the station.' He looked fondly at the little Italian. 'Now the boys run the station and

Angelo and his wife can do what they love. Cook. Here he comes.'

Andy stood up and Angelo pumped Andy's hand as if he'd never let it go.

'Dr Andy, and your beautiful lady.'

'This is Montana, Angelo.'

'Welcome, Signorina Montana, to our Paragon.'

Montana didn't like to say she was a signora. Especially as Andy didn't correct the man. She felt unmarried tonight.

Angelo placed two menus on the table and leaned towards Montana as if he had a secret to share. 'He saved my life, this doctor. A snake bite. And so fast he gives the anti-venom, arranges for my transfer to Brisbane, and I survive. I would be dead but for him. But here I am and my beautiful wife and I will prepare you food from the gods.'He paused and spread his arms. 'What's mine is yours.' He beamed at them both. 'Now, tell me, Andy, who is this beautiful lady?'

'Montana is a midwife. Perhaps your son's sons can be born at the Lake now that she is here.'

'Ah. Si. This would be excellent.' He nodded and smiled again, dark eyes twinkling. 'Maybe a granddaughter for my wife one day. That would be good.'

Andy nodded. 'You're looking well. How are Angelina and the boys?'

Angelo patted his round stomach. 'I am too well. My Angelina you will see later. She is beautiful, and my boys are multiplying. Already I have six grandsons. How can a man be so fortunate? Eh?' He pointed at Andy and said to Montana, 'Relax. Enjoy. He is a good man.'

Montana smiled. 'I know.'

'I will be back.' Angelo nodded, smiled and left them.

'He's great, Andy. So is this place. I had no idea, judging from the outside, it looks like an ordinary pizza parlour.'

'Wait till you taste the food.' He kissed his fingers and grinned.

After much consultation with Angelo, who wouldn't allow their first choice, they ordered. 'You must be brave!' he said sternly.

Angelo brought them a chilled bottle of sparkling Shiraz from a boutique vineyard. 'On the house. This is from my cousin in the Hunter Valley and I save it for special occasions. For you, only the best wine. Taste.'

Angelo poured the deep plum-coloured wine and it twinkled in their glasses like the fizzing atmosphere that had been building between Montana and Andy since they'd sat down.

Montana's first sip made her eyes open wide and Angelo clapped his hands in delight. 'See!'

'My goodness.' She sipped again. The plum and berry-flavoured Shiraz bubbled and rolled on her tongue and this time she closed her eyes to concentrate. 'Amazing. My first sparkling red and I'm already addicted. I'd better not drink too much or Dawn will suffer.'

'A glass will be fine.'

Angelo left them and Montana looked up to see Andy watching her. A tiny smile tilted the corner of his lips. So attractive it made the warmth steal into her face again and she wished she had a fan to wave and cool her cheeks. 'What?'

'You!' He tilted his head. 'Watching you makes me smile. You make me feel good.'

The words were simple but there was no doubting his sincerity and he followed them with his hand across the table to capture her fingers. 'I'm falling for you, Montana, and it's time I told you that. So, I give you purple roses.'

He brushed the blooms at the side of her plate gently. 'Love at first sight. And I thought that was a myth.'

She could feel the shock reflected in her face and he sat back. Her fingers slid from his and he smiled ruefully.

'It's okay. Don't look so shaken. It's my problem, not yours. I just wanted you to know in case you could begin to think about us building a life together some time in the future.'

He leaned forward and topped up his glass to help fill the silence that had fallen. She glanced around the room to see if it all still looked the same because suddenly the atmosphere was different.

Nothing had drastically changed in the environment but everything between her and Andy had tilted.

She picked up her glass and swirled the liquid, not sure what to say. Reminded herself to savour the contents rather than taking a deep gulp.

It wasn't just moving on from the past, and Duncan, and how she saw her future. It was Andy, fearlessly facing the same and moving on, unlike her. He was incredibly brave. And she didn't know if she could match that bravery.

A big part of her was terrified that now it had been said there was no going back, while another released tiny bubbles of excitement like the Shiraz in the glass she stared into.

'Don't stress.' He soothed. 'Enjoy the meal.'

Andy's voice drifted softly over her, just like it had when she'd been on the mountain, and she remembered who he was. This was Andy. She was safe.

'Just think about it for a while,' he said. 'We're still friends... Right?'

She raised her eyes and nodded her head. He was right. He didn't expect her to respond in kind in this instant.

She couldn't.

With relief, she watched Angelo approach with crusty

bruschetta and the Italian's smile lightened her preoccupation.

They were friends. They were colleagues. She could enjoy this night.

The conversation between them turned to the hospital and the new maternity wing. The hunt for staff looked to be easier than expected now word had spread about the caseload midwifery programme about to start.

They discussed a spate of sick children in the last week and gradually she relaxed and began to enjoy herself again.

The main course was accompanied by a visit from Angelo's wife, a tall, black-eyed seductress. The goddess who had borne four strapping sons.

'And she rules them with a rod of iron. A very strong lady is our Angelina,' Andy said later when she'd gone.

'This town becomes more interesting and exciting the more I see of it.'

'Good,' said Andy, and she could see he was pleased, although he said no more.

They skipped dessert to savour a liqueur that Angelo recommended they try. Inky black Sambucca with coffee beans brought in tiny shot glasses that Angelo lit, whirling, extinguishing and ordering them to sip. Montana had insisted on only half a shot.

The heated liqueur slid like black gold down her throat and Montana hoped Dawn wouldn't mind that she'd had two drinks tonight.

When Andy suggested they dance she knew it would feel different because of his declaration. He stood beside her chair and held out his hand to help her up. Now she felt like a princess again. How did he do that? Create such magic?

When his arms circled her waist, she closed her eyes and leant against him. His shirt was a thin barrier to the firm muscles under her cheek and his lips near her neck made her sensitive to every breath that he took.

Their steps matched in perfect harmony as they swayed to the music. Strange, because no part of her brain could be spared for such a mundane thing as rules of a dance while Andy held her. His scent, his warmth, his tenderness surrounded her.

And he offered so much more if only she could cross those final barriers and accept it.

On their walk home, she declined Andy's suggestion for a stroll around the lake. Two drinks, and a dreamy dance spelt danger and desire. She needed time to consider the implications of Andy's stated intention. She needed time, full stop.

Instead they walked home to Dawn, and with a lingering parting of fingers separated to their own rooms.

For Montana, there was a lot to think about.

Perhaps it was time to consider life after Duncan without the associated guilt. Without apologising for being alive when he wasn't. She acknowledged to herself that she had loved her husband with all her heart, body and soul until the end.

But she and Dawn weren't meant to be lonely and alone.

She needed a partner, a lover, a second half to share her triumphs and her fears with, someone to "talk" to, and she so loved talking to Andy. Dawn needed a good father and Andy would slip into that role magnificently — had already slipped into that role.

She wanted to grow old with Andy and together they would share common goals, achieve milestones to be proud of, watch over and celebrate Dawn. She could see him as that one person in her world to spend her life with. To feel at home with. Be the centre of her world as she would be the centre of his.

She missed being a wife. She wanted to be Andy's wife.

She loved the way Andy had shown her tonight how special he found her. The roses, the romance, his obvious pleasure in her pleasure. The smoulder in his eyes when he looked at her. And she knew he would be a wonderful lover. As generous in bed as out, and that thought brought a flush to her skin that heated her right down to her toes.

If she started to think of Andy's strong neck and broad chest and those glorious shoulders and arms, she'd be a basket case.

If she was honest with herself, she'd admit she wanted to be seduced by Andy. Feel his hands on her skin. Let go and be held for the whole night.

That had been the main factor in refusing to walk by the lake tonight. She'd wanted distance and time before she irrevocably committed herself, and if he'd leant on her tonight she'd have been unable to say no.

Of course he hadn't pushed.

He was Andy.

And the final reason she held back was the realisation that she had fallen in love with Andy, and she was terrified it was a different, more complete love than that she had shared with Duncan. She needed to find peace with that.

# Montana

## CHAPTER NINETEEN

By mid May the birthing centre application had been assessed and passed for their first birth. Suddenly time for Montana and Andy to spend together deserted them.

The maternity wing had been furnished like a home, not a hospital. Montana had begun the antenatal clinic and started introducing new staff to the hospital. All they needed was a woman in labour.

That, along with her administration days, left little time to spend with Andy. Two young midwives whose husbands worked at the mine had been employed and had begun antenatal care with half a dozen clients at different stages in their pregnancy.

Sara and Charlotte couldn't believe their luck at finding their dream jobs. Though not long graduated, both had loads of experience in a tertiary-affiliated birth centre in Brisbane, and were very happy to work with the base hospital whenever they needed to transfer a patient.

Each would work two shifts on call and two off, and Montana would be the second person when birth was imminent. She didn't take any of her own clients except for Emma.

More midwives were needed but there was no hurry. Montana doubted they would be run off their feet in the beginning, even with the rapid population growth from the mine.

By June, Sara and Charlotte had accepted two more women each on their caseloads, which meant the women visited the unit for antenatal care with more visits as they drew closer to their due dates. As yet they hadn't had reason to pass any women with complications to Andy to refer on to the base obstetricians.

The first baby was due at the end of June and the three midwives carried their mobile phones everywhere, even where reception proved tricky.

Andy had offered to take Dawn into his room at night if she was called out for any births and Louisa had been eager to cover in daytime. Montana was still breast-feeding Dawn but ensured she had enough expressed breast milk frozen to cover contingencies.

Today was Emma's antenatal visit in the new clinic. 'So how are you keeping, Emma? Two weeks to go?' Montana let down the blood-pressure cuff on Emma's arm as she studied her face.

Emma shrugged miserably. 'I'm okay. Baby kicks a lot and now I'm getting heartburn after I eat. And that's most of the time.'

'Heartburn is horrible. When you have your baby that will go away. In the meantime, try smaller meals. Sometimes, giving your tummy time to empty before you drink anything new, helps. That will stop the acid contents splashing up through the floppy door leading from your tummy into your throat.'

'Gross. Why have I got a floppy door now?' Emma

sounded fed up and Montana sympathised with the tiredness of late pregnancy.

'It's all the fault of those muscle-loosening hormones. Your body can't pick and choose between muscles in your pelvis and muscles in your stomach, but your body is preparing itself for birth. Remember you can hurt your back easily now, too, as muscles can over-stretch.'

'I'm sick of me. Can we change the subject? How's Dawn?' Emma wanted to know. She had become very fond of Montana's baby over the past months.

Montana smiled. 'She's rolling over onto her tummy and back again and puts everything into her mouth. And she loves having conversations with Andy. He talks, she gurgles and then he talks and she shrieks. It's so funny. You'll have to come and visit again.'

'I'd like that.'

'You and Tommy are coming to the class tonight, aren't you?'

'You bet. I want to see Andy in front of a class.'

That night Montana ran the first antenatal night class ever in Lyrebird Lake, with four women and their partners as well as Emma and Tommy on a revision course.

The session had proved popular, especially as the partners had never had the chance to attend before in town.

Montana discussed normal labour and Andy gave descriptions of labour complications from the medical aspect. They discussed reasons for transfer out of the centre to the base hospital and talked about premature labour and antenatal medical complications as well.

By the end of the session even Tommy said he was glad he'd come. She hoped he'd feel the same next week.

The first of July heralded cooler weather and when Montana carried Dawn into a late breakfast, Andy's big cheesy grin meant he had a surprise for them both. When she saw the pink balloons around Dawn's high chair and a handmade card on her little tray table, she didn't understand the significance.

'Happy birthday, Dawn.' The others clapped as Montana carried her daughter in.

'You're all mad,' she said from just inside the doorway. 'It's not her birthday for another six months.'

Andy sniffed. 'It's her half-birthday and it's the first of July. I declare a Lyrebird Lake holiday because it's Sunday.' Andy swooped Dawn from her mother's arms and flew her over to her chair to see the balloons.

Dawn cackled in delight and waved her hands as she tried to capture Andy's face. Louisa stood clapping her hands and even Ned had appeared early to be part of the festivities.

Montana looked around at the warm, caring faces of these people who had taken her into their home. At a time when she'd needed unobtrusive support they'd given unstintingly, and she could feel the sting of tears. Andy would have arranged this. She forced her tears back because the last thing they needed was to think they had upset her.

She sniffed. 'Who would have thought today was such a momentous day? How could I have forgotten my own daughter's half-birthday?'

Ned tut-tutted.

Andy nodded sagely. 'You may have had other things on your mind but it's okay. We have your back.'

Yes, you do, she thought.

Her face split with the biggest smile as Louisa bustled over with a pink-iced cake decorated with a picture of a sunrise and "Half" written in icing.

'Oh, my!' Montana peered at the cake. 'Louisa, that is a work of art. It is so beautiful; I have to take a photo! But won't we all be sick if we have that for breakfast?'

'You could squeeze in a wee piece if you eat it after eggs,' Ned declared sagely.

Even Dawn enjoyed her cake by mushing it gloriously between her fingers, finger-painting her tray and then smearing icing and crumbs all over her face. Her little pink tongue darted busily as she crowed and played with her unexpected treat.

Louisa hovered with a dishcloth, not sure how far and wide Dawn was capable of spreading the mess, while the others backed off. Montana savoured the moment. Madness, silliness, and the love behind it all.

After the party, Andy tucked Dawn against his side and drew Montana out onto the veranda and into the swing seat. The three of them swung gently and gazed across the lake. 'So where would you like to go for Dawn's birthday?' Andy asked.

'A half-birthday outing? Does this day get even better?' she teased.

Andy's eyes darkened wickedly and she blushed and looked away. They really hadn't had time for themselves and she knew Andy wanted to talk again about their future. It was time she met him halfway.

'We'd love a picnic.' Montana gestured across at the lake and then up to the hills. 'I hear there's a waterfall halfway down the creek. A doctor/pilot I met once,' she cast him a teasing sidelong glance 'told me there was a waterfall in the hills. One you can walk to town from or park up near the old mine.'

'It is a pretty spot,' the doctor/pilot said, 'but it's quite a hike, especially carrying a hamper and a half-year-old baby. I think we should drive. There's a great clearing not far from the old antimony mine with a swimming pool nearby.'

Montana's smile spread with delight. Dawn would love her first picnic. 'Sounds perfect. Are you on call?'

Andy nodded. 'But higher up there's decent mobile service. Hopefully I won't get called away before we eat. I'm looking forward to the cake.'

Montana patted her stomach. 'I won't be eating much more cake if I want to fit into my jeans.'

Andy raised his eyebrows in mock censure. 'There's always room for the good things in life.'

'Like cake?'

'Especially cake,' Andy said seriously. 'Trust me. I'm a doctor and a pilot.'

# Montana

## CHAPTER TWENTY

Three hours later because like most mothers it seemed to take Montana that long to organise any expedition with Dawn they finally found the waterfall. A waist-deep pool beckoned beyond and Andy answered the call even though it was quite cool. Swimming in July? The man was barking mad.

Montana dangled Dawn's feet at the edge and tried not to stare at Andy in his swimmers, black board shorts that showed off his washboard abs as he encouraged her to join him.

Droplets sparkled in his hair and off his strong throat as he played in the water and pretended to splash her. His green eyes promised wet skin contact if she dared, his lips spoke silly talk to Dawn.

When she refused for the third time he dived under the water and then lifted himself effortlessly onto the smooth boulder beside Montana. 'I haven't been here for ages. I have no idea why not. I'd forgotten how much I love it.'

He was close and wet and half-naked and she wanted to

chase rivulets of water down his chest just to feel the firmness beneath her fingers. Just to touch him.

Instead she said, 'It's good to see you relaxed. You work so hard week in, week out. How do you keep your good humour? That's what I want to know.'

'Great friends. Great people.' He shrugged. 'It's not hard when you love your work.'

She realised his kindness never seemed stretched. It seemed to come effortlessly to him. Like today and the party he'd organised for Dawn.

'You should have more time off, Andy,' she said. 'Look after yourself, instead of arranging parties for stray mothers and babies.'

He smiled crookedly. 'I will when I have a reason to take time off.'

The words were offered lightly but Montana knew they were directed at her and suddenly the little oasis seemed warmer and more private. She felt the honesty of his words and accepted his ability to say out loud what he wanted, yet in a way to save her from feeling awkward. A step in the right direction that she could at least acknowledge to herself.

Still, she shifted topic to allow herself time to adjust. 'How did you remember it was Dawn's half-birthday?'

'You're kidding me, right?' Andy shook his head, denying it had been hard. 'How could I forget the day you and Dawn came into my life?'

'It was a memorable day,' she said.

Andy looked across at her baby, dozing now on her mother's lap. 'I could never forget the magic on the mountain on New Year's Day?' he added softly, and his words brought back the serenity of that morning. Then he leant across and kissed her cheek and she could see he really did remember that day with emotion. 'You were amazing.'

She looked at this wonderful, caring man beside her. A man who offered her the sort of connection she missed so dreadfully. She said softly, 'And you came to save me. Driving up a strange mountain in the early morning mist because your sister asked a favour for her friend. You brought me a hot water bottle and warmed my feet. Gave me Jasmine tea in a cozy car and cuddled my new baby until I was ready to go. You were pretty amazing yourself, Dr Buchanan.'

She found herself leaning towards him as his long fingers splayed across her cheek. The caress of his thumb along her jawline sent wild sensations tumbling into her stomach and chest. She closed her eyes. She didn't see his mouth coming, but she waited, knowing it would happen.

Wanting it to happen.

Strong arms drew her nearer until she was snug against his taut body. His lips brushed at hers with gently swooping caresses until he captured her in a timeless seduction that drew the breath from her in tiny gasps of air.

Somehow her fingers buried in his hair in a quest to stay connected with his mouth.

The world receded into seductive sensation but Dawn didn't like the lack of attention. She squirmed in Montana's lap and the moment drifted away, as did Andy's mouth, and Montana sat back. Bereft.

'Perhaps you should go to your room,' he said softly to Dawn, and nodded at the pram mock-sternly. 'Your mother and I are talking.'

He stood up. Gathered his clothes. 'I guess it is her birthday, not mine. I'll dress then help you unpack the hamper.'

Montana watched him go and wondered at his patience with Dawn. His patience with her. Maybe he was too patient?

They spent the rest of the afternoon discussing their childhoods and important people in their lives while Dawn played happily with shiny stones she couldn't pick up, and watched the activity of the trees and the tiny animals around the pool.

Montana felt the shift in their relationship, the brighter smile on Andy's face, his brushing of her hand and her own need to grasp his fingers when he did. The nuances were subtle but strong, and she smiled with the rightness of moving forward with a man she trusted and admired. And just maybe had grown to love.

At two, they packed and drove home and not long after Andy went out on a call to the hospital.

Montana dozed with Dawn on the big bed in her room, but pictures and memories of Andy crowded her mind. Was she wasting her life? Could she be happy with Andy? Would Andy love Dawn as a father?

Yes, of course. To each and every question. So why, why couldn't she just say yes to moving forward in her relationship with Andy? Why this ridiculous hesitation and crushing load of guilt about Duncan?

Again, she examined the concept that seeing the differences between Duncan and Andy was not a disloyalty. She could love them both. It wasn't that she hadn't loved Duncan as she realised she loved Andy, and those differences shouldn't make her feel unfaithful to her dead husband.

The real fear emerged from a dark place inside her. If it had almost killed her to lose Duncan, what if she married Andy and fell more deeply in love every minute?

What of her soul should anything happen to Andy?

How would she ever survive?

The clarity of that fear had her sitting up on the edge of the bed with her heart pounding in her chest. Maybe that fear was larger than the fear of loneliness and of forgetting Duncan. It was scary to think it might be.

She buried her head under her pillow and her fingers crept around Dawn's little sleeping body for comfort. She was in trouble whatever she did.

The phone call came through at four-thirty in the afternoon from Emma's boyfriend, Tommy. It took Montana a moment to connect pregnant Emma and her baby's father.

'Montana?' His voice faded in and out with poor reception and Montana walked to the window.

'Tommy, is that you?' She couldn't rationalise the reason but a cold chill ran down her neck at the sound of his worried voice.

'Emma's missing. I've looked and looked.'

Montana frowned. 'What do you mean, missing?'

'She went for a walk from her parent's house and didn't come back.' There was that thread of panic again in Tommy's voice that tweaked her own worry.

Montana glanced at the clock. 'Have you told her father?'

'He's at the mill with her brothers and they don't have good phone service out there in the bush. I can't get through to him.' Tommy paused and then the words came in a rush. 'She's been acting strange and I'm worried.'

'I'm sure she's fine, Tommy.' Montana squeezed the phone in her hand until her fingers whitened. 'Probably just forgot the time.'

'She left after breakfast and she's not back yet. She didn't take anything to eat.'

The dread inside Montana increased. 'Your phone is on private. Give me your number and I'll ring you back.'

Montana tried Andy's mobile but he was out of range, and

when she tried the hospital Chrissie said he was in a distant gully visiting an old man in a shack.

Ned had a distressed patient so she couldn't ask his advice and even Bob, the policeman, had been out when she rang. Montana didn't know who else to contact.

She rang Tommy back. 'Did she say where she was going? Or give any hints?'

'Just that she needed to go for a walk. She can't have gone far 'cause she's pretty big and waddles. She likes to sit in the gully near the mine because there's a creek but I looked there already.'

Montana tried to think. 'Have you rung all her friends?'

'Yep. Even the unfriendly ones. Nobody has seen her today.' Tommy had actually done very well with his sleuthing.

Montana's brain raced. 'Was she upset when you talked to her this morning?'

'Yep,' he said. 'She's been getting queerer every day.'

Awesome. Montana felt like shaking him and asking why he hadn't mentioned something before this.

But that wouldn't help and she needed Tommy thinking clearly, not upset by her censure. 'Fine. I'll have a drive around, Tommy, and see if I can find her. Do you know if she has her mobile phone?'

'No.' Brief and non-explanatory, and she waited for him to elaborate. He didn't.

Frustration had her grit her teeth. 'No, she doesn't have her phone or, no, you don't know?'

'Don't know.' Tommy began to sound frightened at the unmistakable bite of concern in Montana's voice.

'Fine.' Montana drew a deep breath and calmed her urge to scream. 'I'll send a message to Andy with your number and he'll ring you as soon as he's back in mobile range. Make sure you stay somewhere you can be contacted.'

She ran through the options in her mind. 'Tell him what you've told me and that I'm driving to the mine. I'll park my car and walk back to town from there. You start from the bottom up with Andy. It will be dark soon. I'd better get started.'

The relief in Tommy's voice was palpable. 'Thanks, Montana.'

Montana rubbed her neck, a trait she'd obviously picked up from Andy. 'You did the right thing, ringing me, Tommy. Now, stay in range so Andy can contact you.'

After unburdening to Louisa, who took Dawn and offered the use of her car, Montana drove back to the mine parking area. Two visits in one day to a place she'd never seen before, although the differences between the two excursions could not have been greater. Today was plain crazy.

She locked the car and began to walk along the rough path beside the creek towards town. At least she had the downhill run. That helped with the physical stress, but not the load of worry on her mind.

What if Emma had gone into labour?

What if she was stuck somewhere alone and in pain?

She would be frightened for herself and her baby.

Montana couldn't help recalling her own labour with Dawn. Running away from emotional turmoil to the cabin and her labour's unexpected beginning. She remembered being alone and too far from help.

But as a midwife she at least had knowledge and experience to fall back on. Emma was sixteen and alone. And carrying the added burden of her mother's diagnosis.

Montana's stress levels rose the further she walked.

She remembered Tommy's words. 'She's been getting

queerer ever minute.' Surely Emma hadn't become so despondent she thought of harming herself.

～

Montana found Emma, tear-stained and terrified, just as the sun went down, midway between the mine and town. She'd twisted her ankle and her waters had broken.

Montana gathered her in her arms and hugged her, so pleased to see her alive, because she'd been having some dark and dismal thoughts as she'd called out in the bush and got no response.

'I went for a walk. Mum told me today that she'd known her nana had had Huntington's and she'd blocked it out. We had a fight when I asked why she didn't tell me earlier. I mean, how can you block something that big?'

'Poor Emma.' Montana squeezed her hand and kept her own counsel on the question about her nana. Most important thing right now was calming Emma, reducing her stress level.

'I wish I hadn't come out here. I just got so scared for my baby and I wanted to get away and think, in a place where I could let go and cry in peace without people trying to cheer me up.' Big, damp eyes and tear-stained cheeks turned to Montana, imploring her to understand, to not judge and come up wanting. 'I didn't think the baby would come today. You understand don't you, Montana?'

'Yes. Yes, I do.'

How could she not? Although the timing sucked.

Emma clutched Montana's hand and pushed it low down on her stomach. 'I haven't had any real pains yet but the five-minute tightenings are getting worse. It's awfully sore in here.'

Montana spread her fingers around Emma's belly button

and felt the tautness rock hard against her hand. It felt like a contraction to her.

She peered at her watch in the gathering gloom. Five-thirty. It would be pitch black by six.

'We need to contact Andy.' Montana drew her phone from her jeans.

Emma nodded her head vigorously. 'Yes, please.'

Montana tried and then stood up and tried again. No signal. *Blast*! She resisted the impulse to throw the useless phone into the creek.

'Look, Emma, I'll have to climb back up the hill and try for coverage, Okay?'

'*No*. Don't leave me.' Emma turned a tear and dirt streaked face towards her and clutched Montana's hand. The fear in her eyes twisted Montana's heart.

'It's okay, Em. I'm not leaving you.' She eased her hand out of Emma's. 'I'll be five minutes, maximum ten. I'll talk to Andy and scoot down to you again. Can you cope with that?'

Emma swallowed. 'Okay. But don't be longer, 'cause I'm scared and I need you here.'

Montana kissed the top of her head. 'I'll be as quick as I can. Sit on the rug I brought. At least it will keep the damp-ness from the ground getting to you.'

'Don't turn your own ankle,' Emma said with a weak attempt at practical advice.

Montana smiled. 'You're terrific. Back soonest.'

Montana jogged up the path and tried not to think about all the spiders that would be preparing their webs for the night. After only a few minutes of uphill slog she had one bar of reception on her phone and she sent a little prayer of thanks skywards.

When she pressed in Andy's number the engaged signal

had her mumbling under her breath in frustration. She disconnected and climbed a few feet higher.

Unexpectedly the phone rang in her hand and, startled, she jerked so violently the instrument slid from her fingers and fell to the ground. It bounced down between two rocks into a crevice just out of reach. Then it rang again.

'Damn,' she muttered while thinking something stronger. She'd have to lie down on the ground and slide her arm between the rocks and feel around for the phone. Her skin crawled at the thought of what else could be lurking in the dark.

'I don't believe this,' she said out loud as the phone rang again, but the glow from the screen helped and the vibration made it easy to pick the right object.

She shuddered as she stood up and brushed herself down with one hand as she swiped to answer with her other.

'Montana?' Andy's voice echoed reassuringly in her ear, and she'd never been so pleased to hear anybody's voice. She drew a deep breath to calm her racing heart.

'Andy.' She had to take another breath before she could speak. 'I've found her. She's fine but five minutes away from me with no reception so I have to get back to her.'

'Montana. Are *you* all right?'

'*Now* I am. Just dropped the phone down a dark hole and had to fish it out.' She shuddered again. 'Yuk.'

'Nasty.' She could hear the smile in his voice. 'Well done. Where are you?'

She shut her eyes for a moment and pictured Emma's location. 'It took me thirty minutes to walk from the mine down the hill along the creek. We're beside the creek and she's hurt her ankle and can't walk.'

Montana paused. He'd love this. Not.

'To add, she's ruptured her membranes and contracting every five minutes.'

There was a moment's silence while he digested that information. Then he said, 'Of course she has. I'm trying to think who this reminds me of?' There was a sound like Arghhh but it was muffled as if he'd put his hand over the phone. 'We do have moments of unusual interest.'

Understatement. Of the year.

Then he went on. 'Nothing we can do about that. I had an idea that's where you would be. Tommy passed on his info and we're halfway there.'

Just like his sister, she thought. 'Family premonitions?'

'Misty would be proud of me. Tommy's champing at the bit to move faster so I'll hang up and keep moving.'

'Soonest.' She looked at the phone and thanked the mobile-phone god for being there. And then thanked Andy for being Andy. It was so reassuring to know he was close.

When Montana skidded to a halt in a shower of pebbles beside Emma, she could see the labour would wait for no man, not even Andy.

Emma turned anguished eyes towards Montana and moaned. She moistened her lips with her tongue, and sighed at the end of the pain, just like Montana had said to do in the classes. 'I'm going to have my baby here, aren't I?'

Montana peered into her face in the gloom. 'You told me you weren't going to have your baby on a mountain.'

Emma sniffed. 'This is only a hill.'

Montana wanted to hug her. 'Well, that doesn't count, then. Besides, I think we'd be better to wait so we can christen our new birthing unit, don't you?'

Emma grimaced. 'Would love to but I don't think I can wait.'

That's what Montana had thought. She re-evaluated their position. 'If that happens, it's because we have no choice. Not a tragedy but awkward. Women are designed to have babies wherever they may be. At least we have a rug and Andy is on his way with Tommy.'

She squeezed Emma's shoulder. 'Of course, you like the great outdoors and your baby will probably be a bushie too.' She met Emma's eyes and hoped her gaze was rock solid with belief. 'We can manage. I did and you will.'

'How many people—' Emma said crossly and drew a panting breath '—do you know—' she breathed again '—who had babies in the wild when they meant to have them in hospital?'

Emma glared and Montana smiled to herself. That crossness sounded like transition at the end of first-stage of labour.

'Um. Just me and maybe you.' She rubbed Emma's arm. 'Hang in there. I'm here. Andy and Tommy are coming. Try to relax and enjoy the fact you'll meet your baby very soon.'

'I'm having a ball.' Emma grimaced and tried to smile but tears began to well again. 'And I'm so stupid.'

'Hey. No more self-blame. If your baby comes today, it's your baby's decision. Do you think it's best to be happy to see her or cross?'

'I'll be happy when it's over. Does that count?'

'It will do.'

Emma flinched at a rustle in the bushes. 'That's the second time I've heard that. What is it?'

Montana frowned and tried to see into the gloom. A little evening light remained but it was too early for the moon and they were beneath a canopy of trees. 'It's not a big noise, so it isn't Andy and Tommy. Probably a little creature frightened by us invading its home.'

The rustle came again and then suddenly, from the bush, a mobile phone rang briefly and then stopped.

They both froze and Montana pulled her phone from her pocket and stared at it. No call had been missed and she hadn't felt any vibration. 'Have you got your phone, Emma?'

Emma's voice shook. 'Not with me.'

The phone rang again from the bush next to them and they both stared. Then a sweet, melodious warble drifted from beneath the leaves and a small brown feathered bird strutted out to stare at them with its long lacy plumed tail dragging behind in the twilight.

He stared, strutted, and lifted his plume until feathers stood up behind him in a perfect replica of a miniature silver harp, just like a small brown peacock on show.

'It's a lyrebird,' Emma whispered.

'He's gorgeous.' Montana couldn't believe they'd been so lucky. '*He's* the phone. They have a wonderful ability to mimic natural and artificial sounds from their environment.'

'That's crazy,' Emma whispered.

As if satisfied that enough homage had been paid, the bird turned and with a shimmy of feathers it strolled back into the bush and disappeared.

'It was the phone,' Emma repeated. 'That's awesome.' Her hand slid down to her belly and she sighed deeply. 'Here comes another one.'

Montana rested her hand on Emma's shoulder. Not rubbing, just resting there to give her strength. 'You're not scared?'

Emma's voice sounded distant. 'Strangely, I'm not.' She smiled at Montana. 'Any more.' Then the pain came again.

*Andy*

## CHAPTER TWENTY-ONE

Before Andy began the ascent he tried Montana's phone again. It had been consistently out of service. Now a busy signal. He stamped down his frustration and worry.

He tried again and this time it rang. And rang. And rang. Something had happened. He moved to end the call and redial when Montana answered.

'Andy,' she gasped. Breathless. He heard a lot of stress and relief in that one word. His pulse rate jumped.

'Montana. Are you all right?'

Tommy bounced beside him. 'What happened. Did she find her?'

'Wait.' He held his finger up to Tommy. Listened while she told him about the dropped phone. Imagined her arms tentatively searching a crevice for her phone. 'Nasty.'

'What's nasty?' Tommy bounced on his toes again his face anguished.

'It's okay. Montana dropped the phone.'

'Did she find her?'

'She found Emma.' He put up his hand. Mouthed, 'hold on,' to the young man.

He listened again. 'Emma's hurt her ankle.' Thank goodness he'd brought the carry stretcher.

His smile dropped. In labour. He put his hand over the phone and groaned. Tommy's eye's widened. He raised his hand again. Listened to the end of Montana's explanation, added his own comments and hung up.

'She's hurt her ankle. Montana said thirty minutes from the top so probably only another fifteen minutes from here, less if we hurry. I'll call an ambulance to meet us here.'

As he finished the call a car pulled up beside them in the car park. Emma's dad had arrived with one of her brothers. They jogged over to them.

'Great you're here. Montana's found her. She's hurt her ankle. About fifteen minutes up. Montana's with her but she's in labour and broken her waters.'

Emma's dad, Chris, paled. 'She won't want to see us if she's in labour.'

'We'll sort it. But great we have four to carry the handles of the stretcher. I have an emergency stretcher in my pack. Those small disposable ones.'

Chris nodded and studied Andy's small rucksack. He ran his hand over his face. 'She won't have the baby here, though. Will she?'

'Hopefully not. They'll be fine,' he added, to reassure Chris and himself. Montana had been fine. Emma would be fine.

He had resources. He had an emergency birth kit, basic medical supplies, the disposable folding structure that they used in rescue, and more than enough men now to carry an adult. He hoped he wouldn't need the birth kit or the medical supplies but having it on his back reassured him.

As did the idea that Montana would meet them.

They all began to jog up the track.

## *Montana*

### CHAPTER TWENTY-TWO

Andy and entourage found Emma and Montana ten minutes later, their arrival preceded by the sudden silence of the evening creatures and then the crack and crunch of twigs and leaves under multiple feet.

'They're here,' Montana said, and felt her shoulders sag with relief. She saw the two extra men behind those she expected. 'Andy's brought your dad and brother to help. Lots of strong men to carry you.'

Tommy followed Andy, and after a hubbub of quick questions, Emma's dad, Chris, took his son's shoulder and moved further up the path to make one call to update Clare. As they left the clearing Emma turned her eyes to Montana. She didn't look at anyone else. Her eyes were glued to Montana.

'We'll move you out,' Andy said.

'It's too late,' she said. And pushed.

Montana wasn't as philosophical about the impending birth and she wasn't sure why, but she was fervently glad Andy had arrived in time.

'Don't be scared. You're safe.' Andy's calm voice settled over all of them and Montana felt the tension ease beneath his composure. Even Tommy lost his end-of-the-world face and stopped muttering as he fell down beside Emma and reached for her hand.

Andy patted Tommy's back as he moved closer to Emma. 'Nice and easy, Emma. What more could you want? If it has to be then Tommy, Montana and I will cheer you on and your baby will be fine.'

Montana listened with relief to his quiet instruction. It was funny how she could handle the thought of her own birth in the bush, but for Emma she was suddenly very frightened.

Andy pulled the emergency delivery kit from his backpack. Good. Now they at least had the bare essentials. And Montana's rug. But she was very glad Andy was with them as she began to unwrap the pack.

As the next pain built, Emma moaned loudly and the sound seemed to ring through the forest. The departing footsteps increased in speed.

Another contraction rolled over the young woman on the rug and a louder moan filled the air as the evening deepened. Tommy's face twisted into a grimace as his fingers were crushed by Emma's hand.

'You're doing beautifully, Emma,' Montana whispered. 'Everything is happening as it should. Here comes the first signs of your baby's head.'

It was going to happen. No doubt. They would have a baby on this path.

Montana usually loved this moment and she glanced across at Andy, who had his hand resting on Emma's shoulder as he gently encouraged her. Their eyes met, a rueful smile passed between them, a shared memory of Andy finding Montana and her baby in the wilderness.

Unexpected birth seemed determined to bond them.

Tommy held Emma's hand, his words of encouragement added as even he realised the birth would happen soon.

As night descended, crickets chirped and night birds called and Emma and Tommy's baby entered the world in a flurry of limbs into Montana's caring hands.

'Grace Victoria Clare,' Tommy murmured on a note of awe.

Shortly after her first cry, somewhere close, the sound of another baby echoed from the bush.

'What was that?' Tommy's head twisted from side to side and Emma and Montana laughed softly.

'Our friendly lyrebird saying hello to baby Grace. I'll explain later,' Montana said softly, and dried Grace quickly with the small towel Andy pulled from the kit. Gently she placed the newborn skin to skin on her mother's bare abdomen so she would stay warm with Emma's body heat and feel her heartbeat. She covered them both with the light baby blanket from the pack.

'A girl. We've got a daughter,' Tommy whispered for all of them, and he squeezed Emma's hand and kissed her forehead and Montana felt relieved tears prick her eyes as she ensured that Emma's third stage of labour was complete.

Andy slid his stethoscope under the blanket and listened briefly to Grace's lungs. He pronounced all was well as Montana tucked the blanket around mother and baby and sat back on her heels.

She stripped off the gloves Andy had provided and glanced across to catch his eyes. She found him watching her, his eyes darker in the evening gloom. His smile seemed a little strained but he spoke warmly to the new mother. 'You were fabulous, Emma. Well done.'

Emma's dad and brother reappeared on the path, their faces pale and silent. They whispered congratulations and awkwardly shuffled down the path again to allow the new parents some privacy.

Andy caught Montana's attention. 'Emma and Tommy should be fine for a minute with their daughter. Let's give them some space while I phone the hospital.'

'Of course,' Montana agreed.

Andy paused before stepping away. 'We'll go up higher to use the phone, Emma. Call out if you need us, we'll only be a minute away.'

Emma spoke up from where she lay. 'I don't want to think about moving just yet. Can we wait a few minutes, please, Andy?'

'Of course,' Andy said. 'But the ambulance will be here and we have to get you down the hill. We'll be as gentle as we can.'

Montana smiled. 'Women are pretty tough, Andy.'

'I've been noticing this lately,' Andy acknowledged ruefully.

'Tell me about it,' said Tommy, still in that awed tone. 'I wouldn't wake up for a week if that happened to me.'

They all laughed and Andy and Montana started off uphill to give the new parents time with their daughter and make the call.

As they climbed, the trees cleared a little and they watched the full moon rise from the east.

'Thank you for arriving on time, Andy, and with rein-forcements. I'll admit to some last-minute nerves now it's all over. It's a bit different if it's someone else who is having the baby in the wilds and not me. Such a relief to see you at the end.'

Andy smiled reminiscently. 'You can say that. I guess I should thank you for the litany in my head as I jogged up here. I kept saying Montana was fine. Emma will be fine.'

She peered up at him in the gathering dark. So solid and calm and wonderful. 'You were just as unruffled and supportive as you were at Dawn's birth. You are an amazing man.'

Andy made his call and they turned back, not wanting it to get much darker before they had Emma to safety. 'Emma is the amazing one. Poor old Tommy will take a while to get over it, I suspect.'

Andy slipped his fingers around Montana's. 'You're pretty wonderful too, you know.' He squeezed her hand. 'We're an excellent team.'

He turned away and preceded her down the path towards the new parents.

Emma became the first inpatient in the new Lyrebird Lake maternity unit, even though technically she didn't give birth there.

Both sets of grandparents had struggled with the shock of Grace's unexpected birth, but amidst shared congratulations, quick but heartfelt cuddles of a swaddled Grace, plus a few tears, all had settled down.

Both grandmothers had been silent as they gazed at the tiny perfect face of their granddaughter. Montana didn't think there would be any more thoughtless comments from Tommy's mother and Clare looked the happiest Montana had seen her. Chris looked proud and stood with the boys admiring the baby over his wife's shoulder.

Emma and Tommy along with their daughter were certainly stars tonight.

Andy murmured to Montana as they prepared to leave. 'Wait until all of Emma's friends see how beautiful Grace is.

We'd better think about arranging a contraception class on the high school bus.'

Confused, Montana frowned. 'On the bus?'

'It takes an hour to get to the base high school and that's the only way you'd have a captive audience.'

Montana smiled up at him. 'I'll bring Emma and she can tell them about sleepless nights and crying babies and no time for phone chats. That should help.'

They both suppressed grins and adopted a more professional front as Sara arrived to take over Emma's care for the night. Andy departed to the emergency department, leaving Montana to her work.

After an extended handover report, because Sara wanted to know all the details of the bush-baby birth, Montana went in to say goodbye to the new parents.

'It seems you're famous around town. Sara said you've had a dozen calls from your friends already,' Montana added with a smile, and Emma shook her head.

'Infamous.'

'No, famous. I think you're amazing.' Tommy stood beside the bed with his new daughter in his arms and stared with awe down at Emma. He turned to Montana. 'How amazing is she?'

'Who? Grace?' Montana teased, and Tommy looked up in confusion.

'Well, der, she's amazing, too, but I meant Emma. I could never be as brave as she was today.'

'You did your job, too, Tommy. You three are a family now. Be kind to each other.' She leaned over and kissed Emma's forehead. 'Try and sleep when Grace is asleep. I'll see you tomorrow. It's a big day when you take her home.'

'That's scary.'

'Remember, I'll visit every day for the first few days.'

Emma caught Montana's hand. 'Thank you.'

Montana squeezed Emma's hand back. She knew she and this young mum would always be close that Dawn and Grace could one day be friends as well and the knowledge humbled her. 'Thank you, Em. I was the lucky one to be a part of Grace's birth. You were wonderful.' Montana squeezed her hand and smiled. 'Goodnight, you three.'

Montana walked away. After such a crazy emotion-packed day, she should have been exhausted but she doubted she'd be able to wind down for a while yet. As she walked across the grounds towards the house she realised that Andy had waited for her. Leaning against a tree, arms crossed, he looked a thousand times more relaxed than she felt.

'Hello, there,' he said, pushing upright when he saw her, tall and caring and incredibly handsome in the moonlight.

She didn't think.

She simply closed the remaining distance between them to rest her head against his chest and close her eyes for a second. It seemed so right.

'Were you waiting for me?' she mumbled into his shirt.

'It seems to be something I find myself doing a lot of,' he replied, his voice rumbling in his chest beneath her cheek. That deep vibration felt healing to Montana.

'I don't mind,' Andy said. 'It's always worth the wait.'

She stepped back and looked into his face. 'Thank you, dear Andy. But you should mind.'

He took her hand in that way he had, cradling it between both of his. And she knew she would always love being held by this man. In this and every way.

They stood silently for a few minutes before he let her go. 'I checked on Dawn and she's just been fed and is fast asleep. Would you like to walk around the lake with me for a little while instead of going straight home?'

Her breasts were full but a walk sounded like heaven. Just to clear the clutter she'd accumulated from the stresses of the day. 'How did you know?'

'You look a little wired.' She could hear the gentle humour in his voice and it drew an answering smile from her.

'That's an apt description of how I feel.'

Already, being with Andy, she'd begun to relax. When he tucked her arm in his and fell into step beside her she knew this was where she wanted to be. By Andy's side. Or in his arms.

They walked in the dimness until their eyes became accustomed and they could see their way by reflected moonlight off the lake. The tranquillity seeped into Montana and she didn't know if it was the peace of their surroundings or the peace of being with Andy. She suspected the latter.

'So are you here to stay?' he asked.

'Yes. To stay,' she said softly, and the conviction in her voice made him tense beside her.

He stopped and turned to face her and she could just make the brilliant smile that lit up his features. 'Forever?'

The devotion on his face brought tears to her eyes. How could she have been this fortunate? 'If you'll have me.'

He drew her against him gently as if afraid she'd change her mind. 'I love you, Montana. I've loved you for a long time, maybe even from the first morning we met on the mountain. I love everything about you and I want to be a part of your's and Dawn's lives.'

She squeezed her arms around his waist. 'I love you, too. I'm sorry I was so slow and fought so hard against falling in love with you. But it didn't do me any good resisting because I do love you. Very much.'

He kissed her gently on the forehead and pulled her against him so she could feel his chest against hers. Never rushing her. But promising more when she was ready. It felt like home.

'You had things to work out. I understood that,' he said into her hair.

She stepped back so she could tip her head and look into his face. 'I think that was what I was afraid of,' she said slowly. 'That I wouldn't be able to stop feeling guilty for moving on.' Her voice gathered strength, from the expression in his eyes and from her own conviction. 'That's not the way it is, though. I truly loved my husband and thought I'd never find love again. If I hadn't found you, I would have thought I'd loved enough.'

She shook her head as she gazed into his familiar face. 'I can see that's not true because you are my future and I love you with all my heart.' The words formed without thought but also with confidence. 'I can't wait for our wonderful future.'

He pulled her into his arms and this time when he kissed her there was less patience and more power, and a lot more passion finally unleashed. He kissed her as if she were the most precious gift in the world and he wanted more. 'Marry me. Soon. When will you be my wife, darling Montana?'

She leaned up and kissed him back. 'As soon as possible, my love.' Then she smiled mischievously. 'You know, those contraception lessons you mentioned would be hard to teach if I was already pregnant before we were married.'

Andy laughed. 'And there is a huge risk of that, let me assure you. We can't let that happen... Can we?'

# Epilogue

The wedding was held on a newly built wooden jetty that had been crafted by the townsfolk and erected in less than a month. Emma's dad had led the working party after an emergency meeting of the local council passed the required regulations for its construction. The white-railed platform looked out over the lake's tranquil water, the first structure on the beautiful block of land that Andy had bought for the future.

Now the future was here.

An arch laden with lavender-coloured roses from Clare's garden adorned the raised temporary stage built so all the townsfolk could see the happy event.

Montana, every inch the bride, was resplendent in a pale ivory gown that bared her shoulders and whispered against her ankles. Her handsome groom stood tall beside her as they listened to the words of the ceremony and every few minutes their gazes would be drawn towards each other and their smiles excluded the world.

Ned played the bagpipes to lead them out after the service and the strains of the pipes soared gloriously over the water.

The sound startled the waterbirds into a swirling formation that should have been doves, but Louisa said was close enough.

The reception was held in a huge white marquee at the edge of the lake with white-clothed tables and children running between the chairs in a lively game of tag.

Emma, such a beautiful bridesmaid in pale lavender to match the roses on the tables, held hands with Tommy, who had a sleeping Grace tucked against his chest in a carry-sling. Excited about their own wedding the next year, they took notes and photos on their mobile phones so that theirs could be as perfect as this one.

Andy treasured the delicate weight of Montana's hand in his as she talked to his sister, and he could see the smiles and sincerity in the people around him.

These were his people.

He was home.

He had his friends and his work, but most of all he had his wife. Montana and Dawn completed his world in a way he had never imagined would happen.

Montana, too, was at peace. The time ahead was for her and Andy, and for all of Dawn's brothers and sisters to come in the future.

On top of the wedding cake, a gift from Ned, a beautiful silver lyrebird oversaw the festivities.

And later, long after Ned had retired, Montana heard the strains of distant bagpipes drifting out from the bush.

The End